FOOTSTEPS IN PHOENIX

What you think about
you bring about —
Think Positive!

Yemi guy

FOOTSTEPS IN PHOENIX

Yvonne Young

Tate Publishing & Enterprises

Footsteps in Phoenix
Copyright © 2011 by Yvonne Young. All rights reserved.

No part of this publication may be reproduced, stored in a retrieval system or transmitted in any way by any means, electronic, mechanical, photocopy, recording or otherwise without the prior permission of the author except as provided by USA copyright law.

This novel is a work of fiction. Names, descriptions, entities, and incidents included in the story are products of the author's imagination. Any resemblance to actual persons, events, and entities is entirely coincidental.

The opinions expressed by the author are not necessarily those of Tate Publishing, LLC.

Published by Tate Publishing & Enterprises, LLC
127 E. Trade Center Terrace | Mustang, Oklahoma 73064 USA
1.888.361.9473 | www.tatepublishing.com

Tate Publishing is committed to excellence in the publishing industry. The company reflects the philosophy established by the founders, based on Psalm 68:11,
"The Lord gave the word and great was the company of those who published it."

Book design copyright © 2011 by Tate Publishing, LLC. All rights reserved.
Cover design by Shawn Collins
Interior design by Chelsea Womble

Published in the United States of America

ISBN: 978-1-61346-088-7
1. Fiction, Christian, General
2. Fiction, Contemporary Women
11.07.19

DEDICATION

From my mother's journal:

>I love you, Father, more every day;
>you're the reason I smile.
>You're life itself
>I love you, Father, for all you've done;
>you open my eyes
>to the joy awaiting me.
>But, God, it was in the storms of life,
>in the tears I shed
>that you made yourself known.
>It was when I was afraid, Father,
>that I felt your loving arms
>wrapped around me,
>your very breath upon my face,
>and your mercy embracing
>my tired heart.
>Thank you, Lord, for your generous love
>that is so real,
>your selfless grace
>that is so constant,
>your total forgiveness
>this is mine
>eternally.

For my mother:

Thank you for everything you taught me.
   Your strength, dedication, faith, and commitment to people have been my encouragement.

PROLOGUE

Kendra was a survivor. She had graduated from the School of Hard Knocks, magna cum laude in her opinion. Having majored in push-me-around philosophy and the practice of no common sense, she felt deserving of the distinguished title of valedictorian. With those two studies behind her, along with some real-life experience, she had somehow managed to keep her faith and learned to never give in and never accept what life threw her way. Her faith had given her the belief that being of divine creation, she did not have to accept Satan's plans but could instead actively engage in things that brought her joy.

Life is good, she thought. *Finally, after struggling my whole life, I deserve it to be good.* She sat on her porch swing looking over the pasture with a smile of satisfaction gracing her lips. The sun was beginning to set, making the horizontal lines of color appear in shades of pink, orange, and red. There were wisps of clouds floating through and around the colors, embracing them.

In the distance she could hear the cattle mooing, dogs barking, and horses snorting, all of them settling down for the night. The slight wind was enough to gently blow her soft brown hair away from her rosy cheeks and dark brown eyes. Her mind raced back to a time when she was a child, lying in the tall grass amongst the white birch trees listening to birds sing and leaves rustle. It had always calmed her soul to listen to the gifts of nature.

Reflecting over her life, Kendra thought she had done pretty well considering where she had been. She remembered when she left her first husband with three babies in tow, having no job, no transportation, no family near, no education, and no money. Her parents had warned her when she had left Phoenix with the man that she would only end up stranded in the middle of nowhere. Not wanting to admit they may have been right, she lived with her choice. She had traded food stamps with the neighbor in order to have cash to purchase diapers, dish soap, and shampoo. She would never ask for a handout, her pride wouldn't allow it. Determined to make her way, she had trusted her ex by giving him legal custody of the children so she could join the military and learn a career. The promise to return the children to her after her initial training was broken, forcing her to remarry him and re-divorce him. *Look at me now*, she thought. She had made the big leagues. She had a good job making more than what she considered big-girl pay with a Fortune 100 company. She had a small ranch, her children grown and—for the most part—independent. More importantly, she had her prince charming—a man who had seen past the barbed wire fencing she had built around her heart and with love and patience brought forth the diamond beneath.

Although her dad had passed away before seeing her succeed in life, before knowing she had found her soul mate, she knew he could see from above. The only thing left in her mind was to work on rebuilding a relationship with her mother. Not that it was truly broken or nonexistent, perhaps just bruised. For some reason she had grown away from her mother over the years. Why couldn't she tolerate her mom? Maybe it was just too many stories that were simply not true. Maybe it was because she never quite measured up, or maybe it was because she was tired of being treated like a baby. For whatever reason, she knew it would take energy with deliberate focus, purpose, and action to build something meaningful there. With life finally good, she couldn't decide if putting in that sort of energy was what she wanted to do. Perhaps it could wait.

In her subconscious, there was a small fear that by giving attention and intentional dedication to bringing her relationship back to high standing with her mom, it might bring too many things to the surface she just didn't want to deal with at this time in her life. Working on her relationship with her mother may in fact show her similarities with her own daughter, parallels of bad judgment one might say. Frequently she had to prevent herself from saying something to her daughter that she had heard from her mom. Hurtful things disguised as "motherly advice." She remembered too many of those comments from her mother to intentionally inflict the same hurt on her daughter.

Maybe I won't tackle that particular battle this year, she thought. Maybe she should just enjoy the peaceful living, her husband, and their home for a while. After all, she felt she deserved it now. Closing her eyes, she took a deep breath and slowly released it. She refused to let her mind ponder on the not-so-right relationships that still existed in her life, the ones that daily tugged at her heart. She refused to think of her sisters and brothers, with whom she rarely talked, or her oldest daughter, whom she just could not understand. Instead, she focused on the good things in her life: her husband, her faith, her job, her animals, and her newly acquired girlfriends; those were what made life good.

Over the years she had found that not every situation required attention; sometimes by ignoring the bad it just went away. Sometimes, you just have to pick the battles you choose to fight and leave the rest to work out as they may. After all, she reaffirmed to herself, if God thought she was not paying enough attention to a particular area in her life, He would let her know. Isn't that what God did? He would throw little, or big, spiritual bricks whenever He was trying to get your attention. *Yes*, she thought, *if I needed to put energy into these areas, God would let me know.*

Happy for the moment that she had adequately addressed any nagging little voice in her subconscious, Kendra leaned back and allowed the swing to carry her into the sunset.

CHAPTER 1

"Cancer. My mom has cancer now. Great! I told you, Sandy, if you live long enough you'll get cancer. It's in our food," Kendra said as she hung up her cell phone and tucked it away. "I'm wondering if Daphne is overreacting. She didn't sound like it. In fact, she sounded like she didn't believe it either. You don't suppose that a person can be so starved for attention that they would convince their doctor to tell their kids they are dying from cancer, do you? I doubt it." She answered herself. Kendra glanced out the window to regain composure. *I'm not going to cry; I'm sure it's just another exaggeration from Mom*, she thought as she turned back toward her best friend.

"I'm sorry," Sandy said when Kendra looked her way.

"I wonder just how serious it really is though. Mom always has something. When she reads about a new discovery in a magazine, that's it, she's got it. She's had it all along and maybe now they'll believe her. Crazy, isn't it? I'll bet your mom doesn't do things like that."

"Not that I'm aware," Sandy answered.

"Who knows? Maybe one day I'll inherit it from her and I can torment my kids the same way. You ever thought about doing that? Just making up something so your kids will suddenly care?" Kendra was hoping the anger and frustration would remove the fear from her heart. "I remember when my dad was dying; my sister Jo was visiting him in the hospital and told me that Mom was telling the nurses that she was a cancer survivor then. Jo couldn't believe it! What can you do though? Call her a liar in front of complete strangers?"

"I have some tissue in the glove box if you need it. Do you want me to pull over, get coffee, call someone for you?" Sandy asked.

Kendra didn't hear her. She was looking out the passenger window fighting back the tears. Sandy was *not* going to see her cry. No one was going to see her cry. She was trying so hard not to remember the same call about her dad, who had succumbed to cancer almost ten years earlier. Her thoughts would jump from her mom's diagnosis, to her dad, to her sister. Her sister, Jo, had also passed away just four and a half years earlier, but not from cancer. No, Jo had another incurable disease she had suffered with since she was seventeen. She died at the young age of fifty from diabetes, an age Kendra was approaching all too quickly. Unable to focus on anything for long, she remembered that neither of the death certificates had stated the real cause of death. Both her dad's and sister's certificates had stated heart failure. She wondered why. Oh, well, she would be home soon and then she would call her mom to see what was really going on, possibly make arrangements to go see her personally.

Kendra was sure she had time. Knowing her mom, she wouldn't die for years and it would most likely be in January anyway, probably the thirteenth or sixteenth so that it would all be in order. Her mom was nothing if not orderly; Dad on the fourteenth, Jo on the fifteenth, and Mom on the sixteenth. *No, Mom would want the thirteenth so she could be first.*

With a small grin she turned back to Sandy. "Want to stop at Starbucks?"

Sandy shook her head and chuckled, heading for the exit.

There was no further conversation as Sandy made her way off the exit, down a few streets, and finally into their favorite coffee shop parking lot.

"What a stupid question," Kendra stated angrily as she began to exit the vehicle. "Did you hear me ask her, 'How bad is it?' Stupid. I mean, really, it's cancer; of course it's bad, unless my mom really does have a rare type that isn't actually terminal. Then she could go on Oprah or something. No, that could be worse than if it were the real deal." Kendra continued the conversation as if she had never faded out.

"That would be quite a scientific breakthrough, wouldn't it?" Sandy replied.

"What would?" Kendra asked, confused.

"Your mom having the kind of cancer that wasn't terminal. Imagine how popular you would be? Or she would be. Maybe you could go on Oprah with her."

Kendra smiled at Sandy's attempt of humor. She knew she was trying to lighten the mood. Having ordered her drink first, she moved ahead of Sandy to the pick-up side of the counter. While she waited for her drink, she replayed the conversation in her head.

Without waiting, she picked up her drink and moved outside to a nice shaded table where she waited impatiently. Trying desperately to reconcile the disconnect in her heart between the possibility of true death and just another ploy at attention. After Sandy joined her at the table, Kendra recounted her sister's words with a sardonic tone. "The doctor said stage four Non-Hodgkin's Lymphoma. I thought that was pretty bad, so I looked it up. I don't know what it really means, but I can e-mail you the website. She's saying no chemotherapy, so I need you to call her and convince her otherwise. She can't just give up. Can she?" Focusing in on Sandy again, Kendra's tone became serious. "Why is she asking me, because I'm going to convince Mom otherwise?"

"I don't know. Maybe because your Mom will listen to you," Sandy replied, still blowing on her white mocha coffee to cool it down.

"She told me that I'm the executor and thought that I would know what to do." Kendra paused and stared off at the traffic, having not touched her drink at all. "She must have said, 'So what do you think?' about ten times during that short phone call. I don't think she really wants to know what I think." Finding a fraction of humor for the first time, Kendra chuckled.

"Probably not," Sandy answered. "Are you going to call your mom today or wait?"

"Better yet, why isn't Daphne the executor? She lives there." Kendra was in her own world, not realizing that Sandy was talking to her. "If this is not some sort of twisted joke, how am I supposed to know what to do? Because I have some vast experience with death and cancer?" Her voice trembled ever so slightly.

"You're going to do what you always do," Sandy said. "You're going to push that emotion off to the side and deal with the facts. It's what you do best. It's probably why you're the executor. Because your mom knows that you can do that, and she doesn't need anyone around her who is caught up in their own emotion."

"I'm sorry, Sandy. I should just go home. I need to process this." Kendra threw her full cup in the nearby trash can and started walking toward the car.

"Hey!" Sandy yelled. "Do you want this, or are you donating it to Starbucks?" Sandy was holding up Kendra's purse and dangling it across her fingers.

"Give me a break, woman! I'm distraught; can't you see that?" Kendra replied, retracing her steps to snatch her purse from her friend. "Geez, it's only my second purse ever and you want to give me grief at a time like this! What kind of friend are you anyway?" she asked, smiling.

Sandy mumbled her reply, "One who makes you laugh—finally!"

I need to call Mom and get her side of the story, Kendra thought as they pulled back onto the road headed home. *Probably have to make arrangements to go out there too.*

"Want to know the good part?" Kendra turned in her seat to view Sandy's profile. "Daphne's calling the family. Good thing because I don't think I've seen or talked with them since Jo died."

"How long ago was that?"

"Almost five years ago." Kendra had regained her composure and was back in her logical mind. "I think Mom's sisters are about the only ones left anyway. I figured they'd disappear after Jo died; she was their link to the family." *At least I hoped that was the case*, she thought.

"How many sisters does your mom have?" Sandy asked as she maneuvered the vehicle in and around traffic.

"I don't know, seven or eight maybe. I never knew them really and never cared to."

"Of course you didn't," Sandy replied in a tone that had Kendra glaring at her from the corner of her eye.

"Anyway," Kendra continued, "She said that my aunt Ruby and aunt Edna are going out there soon. My cousin Lisa is going out sometime this fall. My sister Toni was supposed to be out there recently but didn't show. Mom won't talk about it. I have no idea what happened and neither does Daphne."

"Which one is Toni again? You have so many I get confused," Sandy said. "Being around you makes me happy that I have a small family. So who's calling your brothers, you or Daphne?"

"Daphne," Kendra answered. "Which allows me to just focus on Mom. Of course, letting her call everyone just helps her achieve her unspoken agenda—to establish to the family that she's in charge. Like always. I hate this. I don't want to do this. It would be different if Daph didn't live there. Then again, it could be worse if she didn't. Ugh!"

As they pulled in her driveway she looked over at Sandy. *You're so strong*, she thought. *Thank you for being my friend*.

"What?" Sandy asked.

Kendra only grinned and said, "Nothing. Just thanks. I'm okay; I'm good now. I'll call you later."

Once inside the house, Kendra let the tears fall. There were no sobs of anguish, just silent tears streaming down her face. As she sat on the sofa, she looked out the window, barely aware of the beauty that lay beyond. *It's funny how God works*, she thought. Her life had finally taken on a rhythm that was comfortable, predictable, and calm. She had been in a car when she received the call about her father too. Then again, she was always on the road to somewhere. "Lord, help me stay sane and understanding so I don't make this any worse than it is. I'm sure you have this under control. I don't know whether to ask that it's true so I don't waste my time and energy or ask for it to be another game. I just don't know, Lord. Help me." As she finished mumbling a small prayer, she reached for her phone to call her mom.

Kendra was the youngest of nineteen children and technically an only child. She loved using that line on anyone she told her story. The nineteen were from several families. Her mom had been married three times, ending up with a total of nine children, one of whom died shortly after birth. Kendra's biological father had four other children, and then she was adopted by her stepfather who had six children of his own—it was a typical dysfunctional family. The terms *father* and *dad* were often interchanged in a confusing manner. Over time, though, it had become common to refer to her biological dad as Father and her adopted father as Dad. She could always count on her mom though to turn those around, using the phrase, "Your father," meaning her stepfather, and calling Kendra's real father by name.

Each child had lived his or her own life and had gone his or her own way without a second look back to the family. While it was probably true that blood was thicker than water, she had never experienced it personally. Kendra didn't even know most of them, being the youngest. She didn't care to know any beyond the five that she grew up with, and she barely knew them. She had three children of her own, three grandchildren, cats, dogs, horses, and one very loving husband. Her career was soaring, and she had recently started her own cosmetic business to keep her sane. Living in south Texas was about as far away as she could get from the rest of her family that primarily lived in Michigan, with the exception of her sister Daphne, who lived nearest their mom in Arizona. With the four years between them, one could only pretend they were close, which was often the case.

She had grown up in her sister's shadow. They shared a room, where Daphne controlled everything, and Kendra was not to touch anything. They shared a bed for years. Even then Daphne had controlled the blankets by rolling herself in them, leaving Kendra forced to cuddle up with her or be cold.

In school she was always "Daph's little sister." She had no name, no identity of her own. She couldn't even be another sibling's little sister, always Daph's. Daphne had been president of her class, cheerleading captain, head of the yearbook committee, president of the glee club, first chair clarinet, drama queen, and of course, homecoming queen. In Kendra's eyes, Daphne was about as two-faced as they came. There wasn't an unselfish thought in her head or heart. It was all about Daph, Daph's friends, Daph's jobs, Daph's clothes, even Daph's hangovers. It was no wonder her family assigned the role of Cindy Brady from the T.V. show The Brady Bunch, to Kendra; both were the babies and both had an annoying older sister. Instead of Marsha, Marsha, Marsha, it was Daphne, Daphne, Daphne.

Kendra was abruptly brought out of her childhood memories when she heard her mother's voice on the other end.

"Mmmm-yellow"

"Hey Mom."

"Oh Hey Honey."

"Daphne just called and told me. How you doin'?"

"Oh I'm fine, don't let her scare you. Nothing is any different today than it was yesterday. I'm not sure why she's upset now. I've had cancer for a long time. I've tried telling all you kids that for years."

"I know Mom." *Better to just agree than argue the point*, Kendra thought. Deciding to ignore the potential contention, she tried to stay on task. "She said I'm your executor, do I need to come out?"

"We talked about you being the executor, didn't we?"

"I don't remember it, but it's ok."

"You don't need to come out, not unless you want to."

"Has anyone else called? Any of the boys?"

"Ronnie called, didn't say much. Mathew called and said he couldn't come out unless I sent him the money. Kendra you know I don't have the money. As much as I hated to say it, I told him no, it was ok. And Keith, well, he hasn't talked to me much at all over the years, you know that. I know I was a bad mother, I just don't know what I ever did to make him hate me so much."

Kendra took a deep breath. The conversation was going down the same path it always took. *Perhaps because we never know when to believe you*, she thought. Over the years it had been challenging to keep up with the various stories her mom had told. All the siblings had collectively agreed their mother was crazy. Daphne had told Kendra repeatedly that their mom had to be the center of attention, doing whatever it took to be just that. Perhaps it was the obvious lies Kathleen had told over the years that had pushed everyone away. Perhaps it was the tedium they all experienced to reaffirm her. Whatever the reason, they had all gone their own ways, calling home very infrequently. "Mom, I'm sure nobody hates you. You weren't a bad mother, geesh."

"Yeah, well, I know you all think I'm crazy. I know I'm stupid, but I did the best I could. I always tried to do the best I could with what I had."

"I know mom. I don't want to have this conversation again, I was just calling to see if I needed to come out. Do you have a will you can send me to look at?"

"I don't know Honey, there's a lot of paperwork in there that's your Father's. I'm too stupid to know what's what."

"You're not stupid mom." Kendra found herself becoming irritated and she could hear it in her own tone of voice. "Tell you what Mom, I'll talk with Blake about going out there and get back to you, if you promise to stop saying you're stupid. Deal?

"Ok, it's a deal"

"Good, I love you. See you soon."

"Okay Honey, I love you too."

Hanging up the phone, Kendra laid her head back against the sofa, *deep breaths, just take deep breaths.* Kendra closed her eyes and eventually sleep eased her troubled soul.

"Hey, Sandy, whatcha doin'?" Kendra asked as she switched over to her Bluetooth.

"Cleaning, watching the baby, what else? What are you doing?"

"Driving to work. I talked with Blake and we decided that I should leave for Phoenix tomorrow. I need to look Mom in the eye and see if she's lying or telling the truth. I just don't know what to think. I even thought about calling the doctor but then changed my mind. I'm sure I'll get more details from Daphne once I'm there."

"Probably. It always helps to look them in the eye. Isn't that the joke your husband uses about cutting cattle, something about 'never look them in the eye'?" Sandy asked.

"Yes, that's the standing cutting joke."

"I never did get it, what makes it funny?"

"Because it's when the cow looks the horse in the eye that causes the horse to focus on it to keep it away from the herd. Sort of like when your teacher is looking for a volunteer, if you don't look at them they seem to always choose you."

"Ok, whatever, I'll have to watch him cut cattle sometime, maybe then I'll get it."

"Anyway, back to the subject on hand. I need to get my mom's last will in order while she's still somewhat in control of her senses, or at least in as much control of them as she's ever been." Kendra grinned. "I can't believe that even after Dad's death Mom didn't create a will."

"Yeah, I was telling my husband the other day that he's going to need a will and soon if he doesn't start picking up after himself!"

Kendra ignored the casualness from Sandy because she understood the playfulness one could feel when baysitting a toddler. "I plan to go out there and put a label on everything so there is no dispute over who gets what. Maybe I can use some color-coded dot system. What do you think?"

"I could lend you some of my grandson's crayons and you can just color on the bottom of everything."

"Seriously, you know what drives me nuts? Since Dad's death, Mom started telling us, 'Take what you want now. I'd rather you take it while I'm alive instead of after I'm dead.'"

"I know. My Mom does that too. We'll probably do it as well." Sandy added, "In fact, I think I started it already."

"It's funny; Mom doesn't have much, but I'll bet you that everyone comes out of the woodwork after she's gone to claim some knickknack that was probably picked up at a rummage sale for a quarter!"

"I know what you mean," Sandy said.

"They won't take it when they visit now. No, they'd rather fight over it after she's gone. That's my large, loving family." Kendra was getting annoyed and could hear it in her own voice. *Why do I always think they only want material items?* She thought briefly. "Isn't it funny how families do that to each other? Greed is born in terminal illness notifications, or maybe it's just magnified by them. I'm not sure which. The way Mom collects stuff, there is no telling where she'll say her latest acquisition was from; maybe some rich friend's dying wish was to give Mom her golden knickknack goose."

"Anything I can do for you while you're gone? Will your husband be home to take care of the animals or is he working? I can always go feed for you if you need me to," Sandy asked.

"No, he's got it covered, but thanks. Between him and his barn wife, I'm sure it'll be good."

"His what?"

"Oh, that's what we call his ranch hand since she's about as opinionated as any other wife."

"Whatever! You guys are funny," Sandy replied, laughing.

"Would you mind helping my customers though? I should be back in a few days. I plan to scope out her area for new customers. Maybe even have a party or two. Heck, if Mom is sleeping or isn't up to it, we'll just give her a makeover while she's passed out!"

Kendra laughed as the vision formed in her head of her mom sleeping in her favorite chair, spaced out on morphine, while everyone helped put her makeup on. She'd have to wait until her mom was too weak to retaliate though. Still, it would be funny she thought, as she tried to suppress her grin. "Eventually I'll just go out and stay with her to the end, but for now, I might as well take advantage of the trips and build my business out there too."

"Yeah, and it'll help you stay in a better mood too. You've been such a grouch!" Sandy replied, laughing. "Hey, I gotta go; looks like UPS is here. Have a good day at work."

"You'll take care of them?" Kendra asked again.

Kendra's cosmetics business, or "hobby," as her family liked to call it, had been the main source of positive energy in her life for the past two years. The training was phenomenal and helped give her a different view since she frequently received the same training from her job. Her job took a business approach and her hobby took a people approach. It was the people approach that Kendra struggled with; the milestones were easy; the feelings weren't. Her customers had been patient with her and enjoyed her levity around the entire business. She would make jokes about concealing one thing only to highlight another. She blamed the blue eye shadow days for having kept her far away from any feminine cosmetic experience when she was growing up. Instead, she had submerged herself in the world her brothers had lived in. A man's world was much easier to deal with than a woman's world in Kendra's mind. Men were straightforward; women were catty. That was the basis of her struggle in cosmetics. So instead of dealing with the emotions, she stuck to what she knew best: the business. She figured women would buy makeup regardless, so why shouldn't she make a buck as a result of their vanity?

"Sure, no problem, don't I always?" Sandy replied, hanging up the phone.

She knew that as soon as Kendra was on that plane, a customer would need a product. It always happened that way. She didn't mind helping though. It's what God made her to do—take care of people, and she did it well.

Sandy shared a similar background with Kendra. Not the large family, but the hardships that came with being poor. They had both been single moms trying to work and raise three kids. They both knew the road of hard labor, avoiding groping men, making wrong decisions, and sacrificing to make the world a better place for their children. Neither spoke about their pasts much. In fact, Kendra always focused only on work, work, work. That's where she was comfortable. Where forgiveness was a part of Sandy's nature, anger was the default emotion for Kendra.

CHAPTER 2

"No, no, honey, don't move that; you'll hurt yourself. It took me forever to get that water jug where I wanted it. You know what that is, right? That's my water storage. Brother Thomas had to carry that heavy thing from my car, and you should have seen me crawling around on the floor under that table to get it there. I thought I was never going to stand again! Can't you just put your suitcase in the bedroom? Do you have to move all my things?"

"No, Mom. I can't put my suitcase in the bedroom. There's no place in there either; you'll trip over it getting up at night. I'm not moving your water far, and I'll put it back when I leave. I promise."

Kendra had been there all of forty-five minutes and could already feel the tension creeping into her head and shoulders. The next few days would pretty much be a solid headache. She just wanted to do nothing. It was so tempting to fall into the role of "baby girl," as her mom called her—just sit on the couch and watch a movie, no cell phone, no conversation, nothing. That wasn't going to happen though. Her mom was so excited about her coming she must have told the entire complex. Already several of her neighbors had come by to say hello and let her know how grateful they were that she was here. Kendra didn't understand why they were grateful and just chalked it up to one of the many senior citizen quirks that she witnessed with each visit. Then, if that wasn't bad enough, Daphne was coming down to take them to dinner—to a Mexican restaurant of all things. Their mom hated Mexican food, or at least claimed to hate it. Eating there would just give her mother ammunition to complain all evening. Although she wanted to see her sister, right now she just wanted to rest, soak in the environment for an evening, and then maybe do some light entertaining. *It's going to be a very long visit*, she thought.

As she stood, she took a good look at her mom. She looked tired, older. Of course, she had just turned seventy-five. Maybe she was looking for her mother to look older and tired. Thinking back, it seemed her mom had looked younger after her dad had died. While it was obvious she mourned the loss of her husband, she also seemed to embrace her independence. Kendra knew the turning point for her mom had been the day she had sold the house and moved into this complex. Here, she had her own apartment for the first time in her life. She had hundreds of old people with nothing better to do than walk around and gossip about each other. She could get all the attention she wanted here, and she could take care of them all. In fact, she had done just that to some extent for the past few years. She had run the concession stand for the weekly bingo gathering and often volunteered to cook food for their many get-togethers. As a bonus, she could also have good-looking men come and fix anything in her apartment that needed attention. Of course, her idea of a good-looking man was not exactly good-looking in Kendra's opinion. It didn't matter to Kendra what her mom said or thought, as long as she was happy. Moving in here had begun to help her heal and that made it good.

The apartment was small. Then again, only one person lived here, so it was perfect. It just wasn't perfect for visitors. Kendra knew she had a choice of sleeping arrangements. She could sleep on the couch as is or block the front door, block the television with the couch cushions, and almost block the bedroom doorway by opening up the hide-a-bed. All that work to wake up in the morning with severe back pains due to the lumpiness of the one-and-a-half-inch-mattress folded underneath. She knew she'd be sleeping on the couch as it were, save herself the hassle and her mom the inconvenience. It was only for a few days, anyway. Besides, if her mom was getting anxious about the water jug getting moved, pulling out the bed could prove to be a much bigger hassle than anticipated.

She looked around the apartment. There was not a bare spot to be found on floor or wall except for the main walkways from the front door to the kitchen, to the bedroom, and to the bathroom. Even walking those would take some agility. Behind the front door was a small bookcase filled with VHS movies. Beside that, another bookcase that was almost as tall as the ceiling. It was filled with books, knickknacks, and newspaper clippings. The only bedroom entrance was beside that tall bookcase with a glider rocker and footstool on the other side. She would need to be careful going through that doorway. Behind the glider rocker was a rather large oxygen tank with tubing coiled up, overflowing into the entrance.

She would have to lean over the glider chair to reach the floor lamp; maybe she could hook the tubing there? It also blocked half the entertainment center. The big-screen television sat inside a wooden entertainment system that covered almost half of her wall from floor to ceiling and the entire wall separating the kitchen from the living room. It was rough wood. It must have come from her sister's furniture store. It was covered with family photos in various frames, a delicate ornamental clock, and colored chicken candy dishes. Kendra laughed when she saw them. Her entire life she could remember her mom having those silly chicken candy dishes, the kind that looked like the hen was lying on eggs in her nest, only you could pick up the hen part and the nest was filled with candy. Normally, it was filled with candy corn. How anyone could really like that stuff was beyond Kendra; she thought it was just nasty-tasting sugar. What baffled her most was her mother's fascination with chickens.

Beyond the television was the doorway to the small dinette and kitchen. Once again her mother had managed to narrow that doorway by placing a curio cabinet half in the dining area and half in the living room. It was a beautiful cabinet, with etched glass sides and door, lights on the inside, and it was filled with brick-a-brack, colored glass candy dishes, and crystal ware (not real, of course, but pretty just the same).

For some reason, her mom had managed to squeeze in a hideous coffee table made from what looked like the base of a redwood tree between the couch and the cabinet. It was piled high with stuff. Kendra wasn't even sure what all was on that table. It looked like a record player, stuffed animals, trashy magazines that contained all the latest Hollywood gossip, and a cutely dressed granny rabbit in a small rocking chair lamp.

Beside the hideous table was the dreaded hide-a-bed sofa, which was half-blocked by her mom's chair and end table. Walking in the front door, one had to be careful not to hit that end table. It was her mom's favorite spot though. She would sit there with her door cracked open, allowing her cats to come and go as they pleased. On a quiet evening, one might even find her largest cat, Missy, curled up on the end table.

The kitchen had about enough room to turn around. It was two good strides from end to end, outlined by the refrigerator, stove, counter, and sink. There was a bare spot on the counter big enough to set a dirty plate and maybe the corresponding glass. Every other inch was covered with something: cookie jars, puppy treats, cat food, cat dishes, more knickknacks and cute sink decorations, decorative plates hung on the wall that Kendra believed were a big thing in the 1960s. The refrigerator top was filled with various mugs and vases while the door was covered in magnets. Kendra reached up and opened a cupboard, both sides filled with medication from common cold medicines to prescription bottles of every shape and size. There were even a few over-the-counter medicines that Kendra didn't recognize. She just shook her head, closed the cupboard doors, and walked to take a look in the bedroom.

There wasn't much change in there since the last time she had come. Another television just inside the door, another rack filled with more VHS tapes hanging over the door, a desk, nightstand, a huge dresser with the heavy-duty mirror that sat on top; this one had etched glass doors in the middle and more shelves filled with books. More candy dishes sat on the dresser. Her dad's old dresser was tucked into the corner with a blue Jeannie vase sitting on top. On the floor was the chest her mother had ever since she could remember, then another bookcase, more movies, and another record player. In the middle of all this furniture was a twin bed. *Where are the records?* Kendra thought as she turned the corner toward the bathroom and nearly tripped over them. *Oh, this makes sense. I need to move these before I leave*, she thought.

She opened the closet doors in the small hallway to the bathroom to assess the work that would need to be done there. To no surprise, she found there was no room inside for even another shoe. She was truly amazed at how much stuff one person could accumulate. The bathroom door wouldn't even close because of stuff blocking it. This was going to take much longer than she had anticipated. Kendra stood and just looked around the room. The bed had a frilly coverlet that matched the pillow. The dressers and nightstands were covered with lacy doilies. A baby doll was in the middle of the bed. Frilly pictures of every kind hung everywhere, even a heart-shaped, frilly something that held numerous pairs of earrings was on the wall. The only non-girly item was what looked like a hand-painted picture of Jesus watching over the bed.

"Mom! What's with all these dolls, stuffed animals, and frilly stuff?"

"Oh, I've had those for years, honey. You don't like them?" Kathleen answered, joining her daughter in the bedroom.

"I don't know; I'm just not used to them. You've never had girly things like this before. I can't remember a single thing ever being as frilly as that heart thing on your wall."

"I made that for my earrings. We had a craft night here not too long ago where I helped some of the older women make them too. You don't like it? You've never seen me with these sorts of things because your father didn't like them."

"What do you mean Dad didn't like them? Are you saying you decorated your house for him?" Kendra could not hide the shocked tone from her voice. The idea seemed as foreign to her as women not being allowed to vote or to have checking accounts.

"Don't get me wrong, baby girl; your father didn't make me decorate the house a certain way. I chose to decorate it a certain way because I knew what he liked and didn't like. I loved him. Why wouldn't I make the house as comfortable for him as I could? Don't you do that for your husband?"

Kendra laughed. Not only could she not imagine herself doing something like that, but she could also see her husband questioning her if she tried. Decorate a house for a man? Unheard of. "You're kidding, aren't you? I mean, of course I decorate my house for Blake; I am the decoration!" She laughed. "Seriously, can you imagine me even decorating a cake let alone an entire house?"

"Oh, that's right, I forgot. Blake is the one that has taste, isn't he? I just don't understand why you never tried it. You had a way with putting yarn together when you were a little girl. Why did you stop? I remember you used to sit on the floor at my feet with your ball of yarn and you would twist and knot it and wrap it until I finally taught you how to crochet. You made some of the most beautiful rugs I've ever seen; you had a good eye for mixing and matching colors. Whatever happened to those?"

Feeling a bit nostalgic, Kendra looked over at her mother. They were about the same height, Kendra being one inch taller at five feet three inches. As a young woman, her mother had auburn hair—thick, wavy, and rich—unlike Kendra, who must have taken after her real father; her hair was thin, straight, and brown. They didn't share the same eye color either. Kendra's were so brown they seemed black, and her mother had a soft baby blue. Although, put another fifty pounds on her and a wig and Kendra could probably pass for her mom at dusk. Truth be told, it had been one of the main reasons Kendra had sought out the cosmetic business. Aging shouldn't have to mean turning into your mother.

There was a time not long ago when Kendra had looked in the mirror and saw her mother looking back. The features were beginning to blend into how she saw her mom. Even though her mother's face had been somewhat disfigured from a car accident long ago, the resemblance was obvious. As she grew older, she knew she would look more and more like the woman who stood beside her now. Unfortunately, right now that was not a comforting thought for Kendra. Believing there had to be some truth in the look-younger claims by various cosmetic companies, she had found herself in business to achieve just that—a younger look, one less like her mother.

She could see the mistiness in her mother's blue eyes. The color was getting dull. Her mom's eyes used to be vibrant, shining, and full of depth and laughter. Her own eyes had never held such mystery. She could not imagine anyone mistaking them as the window to her soul. *It could just be a trait of brown eyes versus blue too*, she thought. Brown eyes didn't make such a great window. Blue eyes had depth, mystery, and variations of color.

She remembered those days her mother mentioned. They were so long ago, back in a time when moms stayed home, sewed clothes for Christmas presents, and baked cookies for afterschool snacks. That was a time when her mom was everything in her world. She had adored her mom then. Kathleen would rock in her chair while she crocheted king-sized blankets for the elderly or lap blankets for new mothers. All the time her mom crocheted, Kendra would sit at her feet and play with the yarn as if she were making blankets too. Sometimes she would sit at her mom's feet, and her mom would brush her hair or braid it or just do wild and new hairstyles with it. It didn't matter. What mattered was that she felt loved. She had forgotten what it felt like to have her mom play with her hair. She felt herself beginning to get choked up, the lump forming quickly in her throat making speech impossible. Was she feeling sad it was gone or sad it would never be again? It didn't matter really; neither of them were those people anymore. Clearing her throat and looking away, she changed the subject.

"It's getting late, Mom. Daphne will be here soon, so we should get ready." Turning away, she headed toward her suitcase.

Kendra didn't like the way her mom was looking at her, as if she could see right through her, asking unspoken questions with disappointment in her eyes. *She thinks I hate her*, she thought. *Why can't I see her and appreciate who and what she is? Why must I always compare her to others? I don't even know her. Not really. The question is do I want to? If she's truly dying, is this the time to get to know her?*

Thinking back, she remembered her dad's last days. Even though he was her stepfather, he was the only dad she had known. She had driven from San Antonio to Phoenix in less than twelve hours she was so panicked. When she had arrived, he was nothing more than a shell of who she remembered. He was so small and fragile. The look in his baby blue eyes was clouded and distant, often looking like he wasn't really in there. Kendra could do nothing but crawl up beside him on the bed and take his hand in hers. There she had fallen asleep until a flash had awakened her. *Mom taking pictures of the morbid; she always has to capture the dying.* With disgust in her heart once again, she began unpacking her things.

Kendra heard her mother's barely audible response. "Yes, honey, we should get ready."

CHAPTER 3

Daphne appeared in all her energy and glory, like a famous movie star walking down the red carpet on opening night. She laughed and hugged Kendra so tightly it made Kendra wince as she forced herself to smile and hug back. Every time she saw her sister she went through two distinct and opposing feelings: one of love and one of jealousy. It was an emotional battle that Kendra was used to and could easily hide from any onlooker, most of all, her sister.

"Hello, Momma!" Daphne turned toward their mom. "How are you feeling today? Better?"

"Hello, honey."

"You look so much better than last time. You have color in your cheeks again." Turning back toward her sister, she grabbed Kendra's hand, "You wouldn't believe it; Mom was so funny last weekend when I took her and Phyllis out to Sunday brunch. She was flirting with the waiter and carrying on like she was sixteen again!"

"Mom? Flirt?" Kendra replied sarcastically.

"Of course, it could have been the drugs she took before we left or all that alcohol she drank while we were there. She was a lush, slammin' down one beer after another!"

"That's not true, Daphne, and you know it. Why are you always telling lies about me? I don't even know what it is to flirt anymore. I'm so old I'd look stupid attempting it anyway. You're the big flirt." Kathleen laughed as she spoke. Turning toward Kendra she continued, "Your sister smiles and men jump to her side trying to help her. With a bat of her eye she gets a free dinner, and Lord forbid she should actually pay them mind. She could be married to the president of the United States if she wanted to be. Ask her; she just had dinner with him not too long ago, didn't you, Daphne?"

"That was over a year ago, Momma. And besides, it wasn't just him; it was the entire group I was with."

"You had dinner…" Kendra tried to ask.

"It was great. I'll tell you about it over dinner. I'm driving; you need help, Momma?" Daphne asked as she reached to grab Kathleen's arm to provide assistance and support.

And so the night began. This was a normal ritual between them. Kendra would become insignificant in the wake of Queen Daphne. Each time Kendra would try to talk, no one would hear. Over the years, she had simply quit trying. For some reason, she just couldn't convince herself to stop altogether.

It's not like Daphne was beautiful physically, because she really wasn't. She wasn't ugly either. She was about the same height with a smaller build and a much larger personality, sort of resembling Doris Day at times. Then again, she could change her clothes and her hairstyle and be anyone she wanted to be. Daphne had always been subject to the ebb and tide of fashion, unlike Kendra, who practically lived in jeans and t-shirts. Daphne was always on cutting-edge social circles. It was important to her that she was Miss Popularity. "Never burn a bridge," she used to tell Kendra when they were growing up. "You never know, the very person you snub today could be the one you depend on tomorrow."

"Even if you can't stand them, you should treat them nice?" Kendra had asked in her childish ignorance.

"Especially then," Daphne had replied. "It's easy to treat the people you like nicely; it's the one you don't like that become the challenge. Your words are so important. You never need to fight or let on what you really think if you use your words properly. Who knows what you may need from one of them someday."

Kendra had looked at Daphne then with the wonder of the child. She had dreamed of being just like her one day. That thought was gone by the time she reached the ripe old age of ten, having established at that tender age that she could never trust what her sister said, for fear it could just be a ruse.

Throughout dinner the talk ranged from how nasty the Mexican food was to how popular Daphne was no matter where she went. She was now involved in city activities, helping her community grow and yet keeping the southwestern culture. Preserve the cactus, yet bring in the people for business.

They talked about all the outings they had been on over the years—Daphne paying for this trip, that piece of furniture, or an expensive dinner in an exquisite restaurant with bad food, of course. It was the same rendition Kendra listened to year after year, visit after visit. She couldn't get a word in between the two of them and didn't really want to. There was a time she had tried to compete. She had emulated everything about Daphne. It started with the vivacious laughter, the touching of an arm or leg to ensure you had someone's attention. She even attempted to retell funny jokes only to explain them later. Over time, she had given up the competition and been satisfied to wait it out. A small part of her enjoyed the fact that they were ignoring her. Somehow it justified her righteous indignation regarding her family.

"Kendra, you have a doctorate degree, right?" her mother asked.

"No, Mom, I have a master's degree."

"Daphne never went beyond her associate's degree, and look at how successful she is now. I used to think an education would take you places, but I guess it just boils down to your street smarts. I remember your father always used to say you were book smart, Kendra, and would never have any common sense. Of course, you demonstrated he was right time and time again with those boys you brought home. I don't understand why you insisted on ignoring your talents and intelligence. Does Blake know how smart you are? He lets you get away with being lazy? Why did you get a degree if you weren't going to use it?"

"Blake is the reason I have my degrees. No, he doesn't let me get away with being stupid, but then again, I don't try to get away with anything. I just do what I need to do is all, and I do use my degrees; I work in that field!"

Kendra knew that her mom meant no harm in all the questions and summations. Still, somehow, it hurt. Daphne was not one to be easily ignored or to allow the conversation to stray from her own agenda. With the pretend love of an older sister that showed how much she genuinely cared, she jumped in to defend her baby sister. "Mom, that's not fair! Kendra has common sense. She's done a lot with her life. She has a good job and a great family. You know you simply adore those kids of hers! Besides, if she wasn't smart, you wouldn't want her as your executor." Turning toward her sister and reaching out to hold her hand, Daphne managed to put genuine love and concern in her tone. "Don't worry, Kendra; I'll help you as much as possible. I'm out here, so I can do a lot for you. I can't really be taking Mom back and forth all the time because it's over an hour's drive one way. You'll be coming back out soon to stay, right? Will your job let you? Will Blake miss you? It's okay, isn't it? What do you think?"

How can she do that in one breath? Kendra thought. Exasperated, she replied as simply and directly as possible. "Yes, I'll come out and stay. No, don't know when. And you know I always appreciate your help, Daphne. I'll be counting on you, as a matter of fact." With a slight whisper out the corner of her mouth, she mumbled, "After all, I'll need to hear some truth!"

"I may adore those kids, but look at how they turned out. Jarred is the best one of the lot. Janie is not just going to repeat every mistake her mother ever made; she's going to take it to a new level. My God, Daphne, you should have seen her house; Jimmy Dean's pen is cleaner than her home. And, Jenny, I thought she was going to be the death of your sister Jo. You wouldn't believe some of the things she used to call and tell me about that girl. Just like her father, that one. What a shame too; she's so beautiful, but that attitude won't get a guy to look at her twice!"

"Mom, stop it." Daphne said. "That's not nice, and I'm sure it's not entirely true. I mean, Jenny is a sweetheart. She's so loving and caring. She might hug you to death. And don't take it out on her that her father is no good. She'll be something, you watch."

"Oh, I don't blame her; she can't help where she comes from," Kathleen added in a softer tone.

Kendra knew better than to get involved in this particular conversation after trying to defend her daughter over the years; she knew it would only give her mom more fuel if she said anything. Kendra knew the truth, and that's what mattered most. While it was true that Jenny had been challenging as a child, as an adult, she was the most solid of all the kids. She was in the navy, knew how to save her money, took good care of herself, and had always enforced her values, never compromising. Even in high school Jenny had refused to be around anyone who did not respect her by swearing or cussing in her presence. And it was also true that the summer she had spent with her aunt Jo had been hard on all of them. Jenny was just too strong-minded and stubborn, to put it gently. Of course, she was that way before she was even born, being three weeks late.

Janice, whom was nicknamed Janie, was another story. Kendra just couldn't find it in her anywhere to try to defend Janie. The truth was, her house was a mess. In fact, saying it was a mess was too gentle of a word, and saying it was a pigpen could be too gentle as well. It was just downright nasty. Not that Kendra would ever say a word to her about it. If she did, she might never see her grandkids again.

It was easy to see why she thought Jarrod was the best of the bunch. He was always spiritual, quiet, supportive, and fun to be around. Of course, growing up in a house full of women may have had some influence on his disposition.

Her mom stood up. "I have to pee, and then I'm ready to go home," she announced.

Daphne looked exasperated. Kendra started to gather her things, finish her water, and was about to follow her mom when Daphne grabbed her arm.

"How do you think she looks?" she asked.

"Well, I haven't been here—"

"I thought she'd never leave us alone to talk. On the way home I'm going to say something about you coming to visit so we can talk. She's nuts, Kendra. She came up the other day, and she was fine until my friend Andrea came over. Then she was like, 'Oh, my back, I need my walker…and my oxygen…you know I can't go anywhere without my oxygen.'" Daphne mimicked an old lady sound when she spoke. "She had been walking around playing with the dogs and everything. It's all for show. I can't tell you what's real and what isn't."

"Are you girls talking about me?" Kathleen asked as she returned to the table. With the grace she must have been born with which was denied to Kendra, Daphne turned to their mom without a hesitation. "Of course we were, Momma. I was telling Kendra she couldn't possibly love you as much as I do." Kendra simply turned her face away so that her expression of disgust would not be noticed.

The drive home was all about Daphne's animals, her schedule, her workload, and how she wouldn't be able to visit much because it was an hour drive between their homes. Kendra knew that soon the invitation would come. Actually, it would be more of a summons, stated in such a way that both women in the vehicle would leave Kendra no choice but to agree that she would spend time in her sister's shadow, being duly awed by her great accomplishments.

Stop! Kendra reprimanded herself. *Stop allowing these kinds of thoughts to permeate your head. You are not this person. You are not a little girl anymore. You are an accomplished woman. What do they know anyway? Let them think what they want while you do what you have to do and go home.* Surprisingly, the *summons* didn't come.

The next day Kendra tried to have a calm conversation with her mom regarding the estate, the will, and the property. Luckily, her mother no longer owned real property. In going through a stack of papers containing information about the cremation wishes, the cemetery where her parents would be placed, and the will her father had left behind, Kendra came across another will.

"Mom, what is this? It looks like a will for you dated 1997."

"That thing is so old. I thought I had thrown it away." Kathleen dismissed the topic at hand and continued reading her newspaper.

"Mom." Kendra waited for her to make eye contact. "This is *your* will. It's been done legally, it's filed with the county clerk, and it's a real, honest-to-God will. It states Mathew is the executor. Do you want me to call him?"

"Oh, heavens no, Kendra! Honestly, can't we just throw it away?"

Don't look at me like that, Kendra thought. *You wanted me here.* Continuing to stare at her mother, Kendra made the conscious decision that this was going to be a good visit and dropped the topic; instead she offered to drive them up to her sister's house for the afternoon. It was good to get out of the city and the heat. It had to be at least ten degrees cooler in the mountains compared to the valley of Phoenix.

It was a different kind of beauty in Arizona than what she was used to in Texas. Here it was desolate. There was sparse greenery compared to her acres of luscious green hay at home. The mountains were beautiful, majestic, full of life, and yet dreary at the same time. Kendra had never learned to truly appreciate the desert for what it was. She could recognize the beauty and enjoy the serenity and yet still somehow miss the true features and benefits of the land. They just never made their way into her heart like the plush green grass, rich trees, and colorful seasons of the east. Texas didn't quite have the colors of fall, but it had four seasons just the same; even if winter only lasted a week, it counted. Arizona just had two seasons, terribly hot and not quite as hot.

The cool water of the pool outside the back door of her sister's home called to her. Unfortunately, the five big dogs on the deck took away the appeal. Maybe she could swim next time. With as much energy as their owner, all the dogs bounced into the house, nearly knocking over everything in sight. The house was huge and nothing like the structure her sister had purchased. She had to admit that her sister had a flare for decoration and comfort. It was a southwestern décor, and yet it had a nice mixture of culture. The house was decorated with

American Indian artwork, animal skin rugs, ancient crocks, bowls, and antique frames. The coffee table was the most unique she had ever seen. It was a massive Indian drum. The only thing Kendra could find wrong was the lighting. It was dim, not a bright light anywhere. Unless you counted the bar light that hung over the pool table in what Daphne referred to as the "party room." That light was successful in making the pool table well lit but kept the rest of the house looking like the bars.

Overall, it was a good visit. Kendra spent time out in the barn where Daphne had unique animals, not the typical horses or cattle that Kendra owned and was used to seeing in Texas. This was her sister, after all, and that meant it had to be as different and unique as her. Daphne had llamas, miniature goats, chickens, a mule, and a donkey. There was even her favorite potbelly pig that now looked like a baby rhino named Jimmy Dean. It was difficult not to like Daphne's home, and it gave Kendra a sense of peace. Being in touch with the landscape, the calmness of the animals, the smells from the barn, and even the chicken coup filled with chickens and birds brought a sense of peace to Kendra's mind, easing the tension that had been creeping in over the past couple days.

Allowing herself time to reminisce, Kendra took herself back to her childhood, back to a large two-story house that was located in the middle of nowhere, nothing but fields and trees as far as Kendra could see. On weekends, Kendra and Daphne would go try to gather eggs from the chickens. Mostly they gathered baby chicks. Then there were the infamous catfish their grandpa had kept in the inflatable swimming pool in their side yard. Sometimes for fun they would jump out of the window from the second story of the barn into a pile of hay below or, in winter, climb out the bathroom window and jump off the roof of the house into the snow banks. They had fun then as children, Daphne taking care of her while showing her the expert method of jumping on tree branches. Tilting her face toward the breeze, Kendra smiled at the memories. Nature always provided the peace of mind and soul that was needed; you just simply had to allow it.

She was almost sad to leave Daphne's home. It was comfortable and relaxing, much more comfortable than the tiny apartment of her mother's. Saying their farewells with the big hugs Daphne always gave, they headed down the winding mountain road toward Phoenix. The drive back was easier, relaxed. Kathleen sounded sincere as she spoke to Kendra.

"I'm really glad you came out you know. Your sister just doesn't get it. I know she probably tells you all kinds of lies about me. She doesn't believe I need my oxygen or that my back really hurts." Kathleen turned slightly in her seat to view her daughter better. "Sometimes I just need my walker, but I try real hard not to use it. You understand that, don't you?"

"Sure, Mom."

"I'm not going to use it all the time just to make her believe me. At least it's not just me she argues with. You should have seen her arguing with the doctor. She doesn't want to admit that I'm sick. I know she doesn't believe me; she never has. She's an intelligent business owner, but when it comes to me, she can't see clearly. You can. That's why I want you to be my executor. You have a good head on your shoulders, and I know you'll take care of things."

Kendra kept her eyes on the road, taking in the conversation.

"I'm sorry I've been avoiding the work you came here to do. I just can't do the chemotherapy, Kendra. I'm seventy-five years old; my husband is gone; my children are grown. Why do I need to fight? I'm tired. I've been in so much pain these past years, you just can't understand, and I pray you never do. Nobody should have to go through this pain."

"Yeah, Mom, I know what you mean. The last time I saw Jo she told me that even if she wanted to, there comes a point where you just can't fight anymore. Your body won't let you. She was tired too. I plan to come back out here at the end of January, early February. My business is having a convention here, so I could come out early and stay late if you want."

"You know, Phyllis was real concerned about me not too long ago. I got real sick. Couldn't eat or nothing. Then Katie started coming around checking on me. I like her and all, but sometimes I think they just use me." Kathleen sounded sad and alone. "You know, I can't swallow. It would be nice if you could come back out in a few months when I have my esophagus stretched. I forget what they call it, but it's a procedure that will help me swallow. You saw the lumps, didn't you? Remind me when we get home, and I'll show you the lumps all over my back, my legs, and my neck. I can't take the pain medication; it makes me sick. The doctor said I have several years left though even without chemotherapy. Every night I pray that your father will finally come for me. I don't want you to be upset; it's time I go. I'm tired. You understand, don't you?"

It finally dawned on her that Kathleen was being a little difficult, even to the point of being uncooperative because she was dying. She was scared. She was alone. It was becoming real. Although Kathleen didn't appear to be any sicker than any other given year, the truth was, she was dying and she knew it. In fact, she chose it over fighting. Kendra had been down this road before and did not want to argue or plead.

"Mom, I know this is hard for you, and I'm sorry too. I'm not trying to be difficult. I'm trying to be logical and not get involved in the emotions. If I let the emotions kick in, you may change your mind about having me handle things. Then who are you going to depend on? Mathew? Daphne? No, I know that this can be one area that you don't have to worry about. I'll take care of it. I'll rewrite your will using the old one. We can just sign it and file it, and then the other will be obsolete. Daphne doesn't know how to deal with this, Mom. You're all she has when you really think about it."

"Your sister doesn't need me," Kathleen said. "She hasn't needed me for years. It's nice of you to say so though. None of you kids have needed me for years. I know you don't want to talk when I call. Your brother Keith won't even take my calls anymore. Was I that bad of a mother that you all feel you have to stay away now?"

Was that pain or hurt? Kendra wondered, glancing at her mom. *That sounds like inner pain, heartache kind of pain, not the pain of cancer. You're imagining now; just focus and drive.*

CHAPTER 4

Janie looked around at the disarray of the trailer she called home knowing she had settled too much for too little in her short twenty-six years. She wanted more children, just not with this man. She was considering moving home, back to her childhood home, only this time with a stepfather included in the package. She just couldn't decide if living in a trailer that was falling apart with a man she didn't love was worse than living under her mother's rules with a stepfather she didn't know. She wasn't ready to rank Kendra amongst the worst mothers of the world, but she wasn't putting her on a pedestal either. It had been challenging growing up with only a mom. Now she had three children of her own to consider. Could she really move back in with her mom? Even a temporary arrangement would be difficult. Janie was convinced that Kendra had never really had it tough. She talked like she did, but she couldn't have if she didn't understand what her daughter was going through right now.

Moving back to Texas two years ago had been a desperate decision. She couldn't let her mother know that she needed help getting away, and yet, she did. She was certain that Kendra would disapprove of the way she raised her kids. After all, she had done nothing right in her mom's eyes her entire life. It was all about her sister, Jenny. Jenny was louder, tougher, and definitely prettier. Jenny was mean, though, and Janie was convinced that her mom never saw that side by choice. She felt that her mom just didn't like her, never had, and had chased away the dad that loved her.

Janie was scared. It was an abusive situation she lived in. She knew it was abusive but did not bother to analyze the extent of the potential damage. *Everything's abusive these days anyway*, she thought. Her situation was probably no worse than the abuse she took from her mother growing up. Besides, it's not like she loved the man, but he did provide for her. Okay, maybe *provide* was too strong of a word since what he did was babysit for her while she worked, and then he proceeded to control the money, her time, the children, everything—who they saw, who they talked to, when they left the house, and when they didn't. She wanted better. She just couldn't decide if better right now was in her own home or in her mother's.

All the thoughts from childhood were on instant replay as she prepared dinner—another night of macaroni and cheese and fish sticks. This is why she worked as hard as she did for minimum wage, so she could not feed her children healthier meals. She could hear the children giggling and playing in the front room. That sound always brought a smile to her face. She loved to hear them happy. She had not laughed much as a child, so she made it a point to allow her children the room to play and not be consumed with rules. So what if her current boyfriend couldn't, or wouldn't, clean the house once in a while; was that grounds to move out? If she moved out, that would leave her vulnerable to the husband she had left over eight years before. She never had filed for that divorce. Maybe this would be the time for a new start, be free from all these worthless men in her life. Maybe she was just tired and feeling a little overwhelmed.

Then she heard the words from her five-year-old son that pierced her heart, "Let's pretend we're making a baby!" That could not be right; she must have misunderstood. She walked into the living room to see her son and eight-year-old daughter pretending. Immediately taking control of the situation without causing too much alarm, she told them they needed to get ready for dinner. Without question or resistance, the children ran to the kitchen table.

After dinner, once the kids were in bed and her boyfriend was gone out, Janie called her best friend for support.

"Gwyn, I was so scared. I was afraid to ask them where they might have learned that. You don't suppose Ty is doing anything, do you?" Janie confided.

"Janie, you need to get away from that man and out of that situation. How much more proof do you need that he's unfit to be left alone with those children? Swallow your pride and call your mom. She helped you once; she'll do it again."

"That's just it Gwyn, she has helped me once. If I ask again it might convince her I can't do anything right. She already thinks that. Besides, I don't even know my step-dad."

"Doesn't he work all the time or something anyway?"

"He's an EMS pilot so he works week-on, week-off. I think it's twelve hour shifts in Brummley for a week and then he's home for a week. It doesn't matter though, I heard he got hurt by one of his horses. That means he's home all the time and my mom is gone all the time. I don't even know him. I don't suppose you have room temporarily?"

"You know I'd let you move in with me, but Fred won't allow that. We barely have room for ourselves with all the animals, and now his daughter and granddaughter are living with us too."

Janie had met Gwyn shortly after moving from Kansas. She was a good friend, one she had always looked at as having it much worse than herself. Her husband was disabled and couldn't work. His daughter had the mentality of a five-year-old and the body of a twenty-year-old. She had been raped the year before, which accounted for the granddaughter Gwyn now cared for as well. Gwyn was the one taking care of everyone in that house, and she was definitely overworked and under-rewarded. Looking at her own situation with new light, Janie wondered if it had been an accurate assessment. Resigned to the inevitable, she agreed to call her mom and at least discuss the choices, if any existed.

After giving it more thought, Janie thought it best to have the conversation with her mom in person. She needed to look her mom in the eyes to be sure she had her full attention. A conversation like this was going to be difficult enough, and Janie did not want the added unknowns that could occur over a phone. Deciding to wait until the next day, Janie stood in the bedroom doorway watching her children sleep. *They're so innocent*, she thought. *Ok guys, I'll see what I can do. I love you.* A tear fell from her eye as she headed for her own bed.

"Mom, can I talk to you, or are you busy?" Janie started walking into the bedroom her mom referred to as her office. She did not want to get in the middle of this conversation only to have Kendra cut her off because she had a meeting or a customer or something else more important to do than listen to her daughter.

"I have time. What's up?" Kendra responded.

Great, she's already frustrated. Janie thought. Determined to do right by her children, she pushed aside the urge to turn around and walk out.

"I know you don't like Ty very much, and lately he's been getting more demanding than usual. I think he has a girlfriend, and I don't know what to do." Janie looked at her mom with the most helpless expression she could muster.

"I'm listening."

"I don't know. I've thought about moving out, but where would I go?"

Kendra said nothing.

She's not going to offer, Janie thought. *Be brave and don't give up yet.*

"I don't think I make enough money to pay rent, utilities, insurance, and gas for the car. Besides, even if I could, all three kids are in school now, and I can't afford their lunches and paying a babysitter."

"If you were by yourself, you would qualify for free lunches, Janie. That shouldn't be a problem."

"It's not just lunches, Mom. Where could I live that he wouldn't be waiting for me every day after work? I don't want the kids around him. Where could I find a babysitter that wouldn't charge me a small fortune and that would be willing to stand up to him if he showed up?"

"What are you not telling me, Janie?"

Janie looked at her mom, wondering if she could ever trust her. *Can't she see how much I need her? Does she always have to judge me?* Longing for a relationship with her mom and unable to reach out for herself, Janie looked at her mother and wondered why she was even trying. She was not going to beg regardless of how desperately she needed help. If she were more like her sister Jenny, then this wouldn't be a problem. She just couldn't understand why Kendra couldn't accept her the way she was. Maybe honesty was the best policy; she would just need to suffer the consequences so her children would have a better chance.

"Mom, I know you don't understand. I don't think Ty is abusing the kids, but I do think that he's not taking care of them right. I can't prove anything. I just don't want him around the kids anymore."

"What are you asking me, Janie?

"If you're going to make me say it, fine. Can the kids stay with you for a while? Just until I find a place of my own. I don't think he would try anything at your house. I know he's afraid of you."

"Afraid of me? Or afraid of Blake? I can't imagine anyone would be afraid of me," Kendra said, laughing. "No, not of Blake, of you! You know you intimidate people, Mom. Don't act like you've never heard it before.

Can they move in next week or not? I just thought since they were your grandchildren you would want them to stay with you first. If not, that's okay. I'll stay with Gwyn or something." Janie didn't want to do this, not this conversation. She felt utterly humiliated.

"Yes, of course they can move in. You can move in as well." Kendra relented. "Do you think there would be a problem moving? Will he try to stop you? Do you think we need to get any authorities involved? I can have Blake help and probably a few other friends if you need to do it quickly."

And this is how it started. She was already taking control of the situation, or trying to; Janie's resentment began immediately. The tension started in her shoulders, her neck, and then in a blink of an eye, the pounding started in her temples. Kendra's voice was the sledgehammer hitting the railroad in perfect tempo. Hoping this wasn't a mistake, Janie resolutely outlined her plan.

The day had come. Janie's heart was racing as she watched the clock. In fifteen minutes she would clock out at work and meet her parents in the parking lot. Blake was bringing his horse trailer to load the children's furnishings. She prayed that Ty would not try to stop them. She prayed that she was making the right decision and that somehow the right things would begin happening now. She prayed that she would have the courage to face Ty and say she was moving out. She prayed that someday her children would understand. At no time did it cross her mind that there was a day fifteen years earlier when Kendra had experienced the same fears. Although, any other day Janie could close her eyes and hear her own father saying, "Don't leave me! Don't take my children!" She could remember the police putting him in the backseat of their car while they loaded their own vehicle with clothes and toys. Today, though, she could not recall that memory. Today was about her children, her boyfriend, her feelings as a mother—not about her feelings as a child. Not about Kendra.

Today, none of those memories returned. Today was her independence day. Today, she had to remain calm, in control, focused, and determined. This would go fine. She could feel it. Taking several deep breaths and letting them out slowly, she turned toward the time clock.

Blake and Kendra had met Janie in the parking lot where she worked and were driving behind her toward what she called home. Even though they lived only seven miles away, it felt like a different country. The road to her daughter's house was weather worn and beaten. The heavy rains of spring had taken their toll and washed out many places, leaving behind deep potholes. The trees crowded the road as if fighting for recognition. Even in daylight the road looked like somewhere you might find a headless horseman.

The trailer her daughter called home looked condemned and unlivable. It slanted to one side and underneath it were remnants of what might have been insulation at some point in time. It sickened Kendra to know this is where her beautiful grandchildren lived. *No child should be made to live in such conditions*, she thought. Scattered in the yard were toys, broken bicycles, headless baby dolls, and trash. It looked like there may have been an attempt to have a BBQ pit created in the sand not too far away. It could have just been a place to have a campfire and a marshmallow roast though. Knowing her daughter, there was no telling what it was created to accomplish.

Kendra took a deep breath of the morning air, filling her lungs with the moisture from the morning dew. There was a slight breeze, just enough to have leaves rustling above her on branches that seemed to be reaching for the electric wires leading to the trailer. The sky was clear, a light blue with no clouds in sight. Just around the corner, a sheriff's car sat idling in the shade. Janie did not need to know. If everything went well, no one would be the wiser. Both Blake and Kendra felt better knowing that help was just a beat away should anything go wrong.

Janie was moving quickly ahead of her parents; it seemed she was trying to reach Ty before they were in hearing distance. To their surprise, they could hear her loud and clear.

"We're moving out. Please don't try to stop us. We don't want trouble; we just want to leave." Janie looked at him pleadingly.

"If that's what you want, I won't stop you. I won't help you either," Ty replied and turned toward the trailer. He grabbed a few items and left. No fight. Nothing.

The truck and trailer were loaded in less than two hours. The children happily helped Grandpa with everything they could carry. Kendra couldn't tell if they were truly oblivious to all that was happening or if they understood fully and were happy to be leaving. Ty was the biological father of the two youngest, Robin and Cole. She was surprised that neither asked about him, maybe because the children had been through so much already. Funny, the movie *Overboard* came to mind, and she could almost hear her eldest granddaughter, Shay, saying, "We need discipline, Mom." Laughing to herself, she thought, *Oh, you'll get discipline now, Shay.*

Cole, Shay, and Robin climbed in the truck with Blake as Kendra opened the passenger door to Janie's car. Not a word was spoken between mother and daughter as they drove away from the rundown trailer and toward their new living arrangements.

"There are rules in this house, so we might as well go over them now," Kendra said to her grandchildren as the last armful of toys and clothes were carried into their new bedroom. "This is a tiny space for a lot of people and animals, so it's important that we all respect each other and do our best to keep things picked up, okay? Since everyone has school, your baths will be complete by 8:00 p.m., and you'll all be in bed by eight thirty."

"I let them stay up until 9:00 p.m., Mom." Janie said through gritted teeth. "I'll talk with them. Can we just have a few minutes to ourselves please?"

Kendra was tired and feeling very out of control. Her entire house was disrupted and really too small for three children, three adults, five dogs, and four cats. *And I thought Mom's house was small*, Kendra thought, looking at the disarray that was starting. Maybe she could leave and let them work it out amongst themselves. That wouldn't work; Blake would never allow that. The biggest challenge Kendra could see would be keeping the peace between Janie and Blake. Blake had worked hard to build a relationship with each one of her children, Janie being the most tenuous. He was wonderful with the grandchildren, and Kendra was banking on that to keep the household in some kind of orderly state.

It didn't take long to get in a routine. The children adapted quickly to the small quarters and unrelenting rules, much faster than Kendra had adjusted to the noise levels. She had forgotten how much noise a five-year-old boy could make. Every move he made was accompanied with a sound effect. And the girls, she didn't remember girls being quite so chatty either. They were seven and eight years old, and Sandy had confirmed to her that it was what that age did: talk, nonstop. Janie made sure the two girls were up, dressed, with breakfast eaten and on the school bus every morning on her way into work. Kendra would then get the youngest, Cole, ready and wait at the bus stop with him.

"Look Grandma, the cow is licking my hand!" Cole exclaimed. The bus stop was the driveway to a barn with a large gate blocking the entry across the road from Kendra's. Cole loved the cows. According to him they were the best because they had wet, funny-looking noses that made him giggle.

"Instead of feeding him your hand, maybe you should try feeding him some grass or flowers," Kendra offered.

"Grandma, cows aren't hes, they're shes. It's a girl cow!"

Kendra couldn't stop herself from laughing. Cole was good for her. She had forgotten how innocence could make everything wonderful. Cole saw the world as it was: no inhibitions, no judgments, just as it was in all its beauty. He showed his love for rocks as much as he did toward his family. He was good-natured and happy. His innocence brought back youth to Kendra's thinking and to her heart. It helped to remove the daily worries and helped her to focus on what was really important. It also helped to keep her and Janie from attacking each other.

"When your bus shows up, you be sure and shake your bus driver's hand with that one, okay? Just don't tell him that the cow licked it!" Kendra encouraged him

"Grandma, you're silly." Cole giggled. It was his favorite saying.

CHAPTER 5

"This Saturday is my birthday, Grandma." Cole beamed.

"It is? I thought your birthday was in June," Kendra said, teasing.

"It is June, silly! I'm going to be six years old. Do you know what I want? I want one of those trucks that goes around and around and makes the noise of *woo-woo-woo,* and it's red with a big, long thing that sticks up when you want it to."

Kendra and Blake were both laughing as they listened to their grandson describe what they only imagined was a fire truck. Why he didn't just say it, they didn't know. Probably because he had more fun saying it in a way that he thought would confuse them. Most of the time, his method worked.

"Grandma, are you going to Cole's party?" Shay asked as she reached to hug Kendra with one arm while practically crawling into her lap.

"Of course we're going to Cole's party, Shay. Aren't you?" Kendra responded as she gently pushed Shay to the side, preventing her almost nine-year-old granddaughter from landing on her.

"Yes!" Shay giggled. Shay was the oldest of the grandchildren. Her mom often claimed her to be a self-proclaimed princess. Kendra thought there was no harm in that until she witnessed firsthand what Janie had meant. Shay had a way of making the world revolve around her and blocking out everything that didn't. In her heart, Kendra felt the similar pains from when she witnessed Janie as a child. Although Janie had never pretended to be a princess, she might have if Jenny had not come along so quickly. Jenny was just a little overbearing for Janie and had shut her down. Even as toddlers, Jenny was in charge. That never stopped Janie from taking on the mom role, trying to provide for her brother and sister whenever Kendra was away. That too was in competition with Jenny, but she usually succeeded in being a role model for her brother. *Perhaps that is part of being the oldest child*, Kendra thought, *or perhaps it was just a case of like Janie like Shay.* .

It was funny how Kendra could look at her grandchildren and see her own family: two girls and a boy, same age differences as her three children, same personality issues—Robin with middle-child syndrome; Cole, loving and self-entertaining; and Shay trying to be mom to everyone. History does repeat itself it seemed. Her being able to see the similarities stopped with the children. Only on rare occasions did Kendra find herself thinking the very thoughts her mother used to say aloud. Not the typical because-I-said-so statements. These were more along the lines of a disapproving mother, thoughts such as *Why can't she see what she's doing to those children?* or *She's going to regret that decision when her daughters reach their teens.*

"Grandma, did I tell you at my party everyone was there, and we had cake and presents and games, and

Mommy made the cake, and Daddy helped me blow out the candles?" Robin was so excited telling her story she absentmindedly pushed Cole out of the way. Feeling left out of the conversation and just a little ignored, Robin felt the need to remind them about her own birthday party just a few short months before.

Cole immediately started whining and pushed Robin out of the way. Then Shay stepped in to console Cole, and Robin pushed her, trying to get to Cole. It was only a matter of seconds before the fight ensued and all three children were crying and screaming at the top of their lungs. Grandpa could barely be heard as he broke it up and sent them each to a specific spot in the living room to sit and cool down.

It was anything but boring having the grandkids in the house. Kendra looked from one child to the next and then to her husband. Blake was standing just out of the children's vision with a slight grin on his face. Knowing what was going through his mind, Kendra briefly allowed herself to remember her own childhood, when she was like Robin and Daphne was like Shay. Shaking her head slightly, she brought herself back to her grandchildren. "Guys, I think it's important to be respectful of each other, don't you?" They all looked at her with pouty expressions and a stubbornness that was all too familiar to her. That stubborn streak was an inherited trait from her side of the family. Suddenly she felt more like Mom than Grandma, looking at her own children's expressions from similar misbehavior.

Finally Shay spoke, "Cole, Robin didn't mean to push you. Just like she didn't mean to push me, did you, Robin?"

"No," Robin replied with a very sour tone.

"Robin, you should say you're sorry to Cole."

"I'm sorry."

Cole looked from sister to sister, shrugged his shoulders and replied, "Okay."

Kendra and Blake watched the entire scene unfold. Yes, it was apparent these children were used to settling their own differences and were quite capable of doing so. "Okay, off to bed, everyone. We want your mom to see how well behaved you've been while she's been at work. Let's see if we can be fast asleep dreaming about parties before she gets home, okay?" Kendra offered as she ushered them through the nightly routine of hugs, kisses, and prayers.

"Hello?" Blake answered the phone sleepily trying to see what time shown on the alarm clock near his head. "What!" He was awake with a suddenness that alarmed Kendra, two dogs, and a cat that had been asleep at his feet. "When? Yes. Okay, I'm on my way." He set the phone on his nightstand and reached for Kendra, holding her tightly. "That was work. They believe the helicopter crashed within the past hour. They've been searching for the crew or any signal since. Seems they went off radar at 2:30 a.m.; their last transmission said they were redirecting to another hospital. I have to go in. They want everyone there, just in case."

Kendra was staring at her husband, trying to put all his words together. Blake was an EMS pilot. He had flown a helicopter in the military until just before he retired, and now he flew one for emergency medical services. She had never thought of his job as dangerous though until now. What did he mean they lost radar? "Did they crash?" she asked softly.

"I don't know. They think so. Carl had just picked up a patient in Harmony and was heading into Holston when they lost contact. This isn't like him. He's an excellent pilot. Apparently Rose was on her cell phone with another hospital making arrangements. Her fiancé works at that hospital. This is not good." Blake was up and getting dressed, not so easy a task under normal conditions, and now with a recovering ankle and this news it became a very concentrated effort for him.

"Should I go with you?" Kendra asked.

"I don't know. No, you stay with the kids. I'll let you know if—"

The phone rang again.

"Hello? This is Blake. Yes. I see. Do you want me to call anyone? Everyone? Okay, I'll be leaving here in about ten minutes, so I should be there by five. I'll have my cell on me so you can keep me posted. See you soon."

He turned with a stoic expression that Kendra knew all too well. He was scared; she recognized it and knew not to call attention to it. She had always felt that calling attention to a man's fears or weakness was cruel. He obviously needed her right now, and that was all she needed to know.

"Yes, you should come too. They found them. There are no survivors. They're having a debriefing in Brummley at 6:00 a.m."

"I'll drive," Kendra stated as she crawled out of bed. It was not up for discussion. The last thing she wanted was for him to spend the next hour and twenty minutes driving to his office alone. That would give him time to reflect on his own part in this scene. Blake was home from work on medical leave. One of his young cutting horses had rammed him into a wall, bringing his toes to his shin. Would this have been his flight had he not been injured? Was he thinking along those lines? If not, she didn't want him to.

After the debriefing there was light conversation, broken hearts, and a lot of quiet introspection. Kendra tried to console her husband at every opportunity by laying her hand upon his arm, wrapping her arm behind his back, or just standing close by. At one point, she caught him by himself.

"How you holding up?" she asked.

"Okay. Tim's taking it really hard. I guess Tim was covering my shift and had traded with Carl. It wasn't even Carl's flight," Blake responded, his eyes looking off beyond the horizon. They had that glazed-over look that Kendra recognized. This was the look when he mentally went somewhere she could not follow.

"Wait a minute; let me get this straight. This would have been your flight then? Tim was working your shift and traded, so after two previous people being assigned to this flight, Carl ended up with it. That proves to me that this was Carl's flight. There's a reason that these four people ended up in that helicopter together. We will never know what changes now in this world because of this; we can't pretend to know. But don't you dare feel guilty over this. There was a purpose here beyond our understanding." Kendra was getting feisty trying to bring him back to her. She could not allow him or anyone to take blame for an accident. She couldn't imagine the feeling herself; she just couldn't watch it on her husband's face.

The next week was a flurry of activity. It was all surreal to Kendra. These kind of things did not happen to people she knew. It was a story you hear on the news, not something that really happens to people you know and love. The helicopter had crashed, and the entire crew and patient had perished. They had disappeared into the Hampton National Forrest; the pilot, nurse, medic, and patient, all gone. It was currently under investigation by the Federal Aviation Administration.

The week began with a service by the company for everyone on board. The experience was beyond Kendra's imagination. Kendra had never really been around first responders despite the fact her husband was one; her mother had been a nurse in her youth and her ex-mother-in-law was a medical transcriber. Still, everything was a shock to her system. The mass of helicopters flying overhead, landing, and circling the church preceded the long march from the landing pads down into the church by the pilots and crews. There was playing of "Amazing Grace" with bagpipes that reached into the depths of her soul and made the entire process almost unbearable. It just didn't seem real. Kendra looked around and thought to herself, *So many people walking like zombies to their seats*. She looked at the pictures near the platform. Large pictures were placed on easels of each member of the crew and one of their patient. In front of their pictures were their helmets, giving it an eerie feel.

The service was direct and yet sensitive to the feelings of the attendees and the loss felt by the families.

Kendra didn't hear half of it as she watched her husband and the other staff from the company. Several people had cried through the entire service, and yet she had not shed a single tear. Then came the final call. Kendra had not known to expect it. Apparently it was a ritual for first responders. The unanswered radio call sent an emptiness through every soul with a longing for a response. There was suspense even though all knew there would be no answer. There was no longer a dry eye to be seen. Even Kendra felt the tears slowly make their way down her cheeks.

That was how the week began. Each day was a service in a different location. The medic was from Cedar Station, which was two and a half hours away from where the services had begun in Brummley. That service was followed the day after with the service in Holston for the nurse, almost five hours from Cedar Station. Then in Harmony with the patient's family, which was about an hour north of Holston, and lastly, back in Brummley for the pilot—a round robin of funeral services that spanned over four hundred miles. Attending five services in as many days left no time for sleep. The emotional drain had left everyone's nerves raw.

The services were similar and yet seemed to take on the personalities of the deceased. The medic was a free-loving spirit. She had lived each day knowing that in helping people live, she got to touch the skies. Her life was settled, she was happy, and she was doing what she loved.

The nurse's funeral was anything but settled. Her life had so many unfinished experiences. She had recently become engaged after waiting for years to decide. They wanted to have children, and then she would stop being a flight nurse. There was pain and regret felt at her services. Kendra could have sworn she saw the departed nurse watching over the events from the back of the stage. Shaking off the feeling, she attributed it to the stress that was continuing to build. And there were still two more services to attend before this would become a part of the past.

The small, personal service held for the patient is the one that touched Kendra the most. As they stood outside the covered area where family and friends sat, she observed the surroundings. The casket was closed with small boats made at Home Depot sitting on top. Gifts had been placed there by the patient's grandchildren. They had made those boats with their beloved grandfather before he had become ill.

The cemetery was small and well groomed. Row after row of headstones lined neatly from driveway to trees. There were a few small bushes with pink flowers in full bloom. Kendra recognized it as a native plant to Texas but had no idea what it was called. The entire cemetery was not even as big as a football field. A few shade trees broke up the perfect line of headstones with a couple well-placed cement benches at their base. Some graves had flowers, others flags, and some nothing at all. It looked like a cemetery Kendra may have seen as a child in the woods of northern Michigan. Her mom used to take all the children there to clean off gravesites, pick up dead flowers, and replace them with fresh or plastic. There was certainly nostalgia in the air and in her heart as she turned back toward the tent full of people.

The family talked openly and freely, not hindered by formality. Neighbors and friends stood in their places to say a few words about their lost loved one. The slight breeze had no effect on the sweat rolling down the middle of Kendra's back, even though she wore a light cotton dress. The countryside was beautiful and seemed out of place on such a day of mourning. The widow was not dressed in black, and it didn't seem to matter. Her spirit was wearing black that day. She sat in her wheelchair staring over the crowd. What Kendra assumed was her granddaughter was holding her hand and talking away in endless chatter.

A man stood in the audience and began to sing a song. He was not a professional, and yet the song he sang echoed through the day, touching the hearts of all within hearing distance. His voice rang pure and true with a love he had for this departed man. At the end of his song another neighbor stood to say a few words.

"I haven't lived here long, and I barely knew him," she said. "I must say, though, you could always depend on him to be sitting on his porch watching the neighborhood like he was personally responsible for everyone who lives here. I could look out my window morning or night and there he would be, sitting in his chair, watching. You never had to worry about anything with him sitting there. At first I thought it was sort of creepy; then I became accustomed to him staring out all the time. It didn't matter that it wasn't any of his business; he took care of things. He'll be missed. I'm hoping I can still sleep at night knowing he's not there watching anymore. Oh, yeah, and I'm real sorry for y'all's loss."

That's when it hit Kendra. The woman speaking could have been her mother saying those words and that could be her dad in that casket. This is what the service would have been like had they had one for him when he died. But he hadn't wanted one. There was just the phone call that he was gone. He had a lot of friends. He was easy to like because he barely spoke. That made it seem like he was a very good listener, and people always like others that are willing to listen. It was only his closest friends who knew his sense of humor, and those friends had to have good hearing. Her dad didn't talk much, and when he did, he was barely audible. The only time there was no doubt in his words was when he was angry, which wasn't very often. She missed him terribly and felt the emptiness in her heart once again.

The last time she had visited their home in Phoenix, he was gone; all his things were gone; it was like he had never been there, except she felt him there. She remembered sitting in the rocking chair with her eyes half closed and feeling him walk by the doorway down the hall. She wanted to say she had seen him, but it was a feeling more than a seeing. It had happened several times during her last visit, which was greatly the reason for it being her last visit.

When her mother had asked her opinion about selling the house, Kendra had been quick to agree with her to sell. She could not understand how her mom could stay in a house feeling his presence all the time. It had never occurred to her that perhaps no one else felt it. It wasn't that Kendra believed in ghosts or restless spirits, but it wasn't as if she did not believe either. It was an area she didn't dwell in so that she would not have to make a decision. She had always liked the idea that a departed one could come back and visit the living, warn them of harm, or comfort them in pain. She remembered Jo telling her in the hospital during that last visit that she would often awake and see Dad sitting in the corner of her hospital room, not that he would talk; he would just wait. It's what he did. It was all good, even cool, until she had felt him in that house.

Blake squeezed her hand, bringing her back to the present day. The people were all walking by the casket, and it was their turn to get in line. She did not know these people or this man and was silently thankful the casket was closed. She felt awkward going up to the widow; what would she say? Her eyes met the woman's in the wheelchair. They stayed locked that way for what seemed an eternity but what could only have been a few seconds. There was an understanding between them, although Kendra did not know what it was. The woman smiled and reached out her hand to squeeze Kendra's. "It's okay, honey; he's with our heavenly Father now, getting things ready for me. God must be the only one that could make that man go first, I swear. Thank you for coming today; it's good that you came to say good-bye."

"Thank you for letting us be part of this with you. It has helped me more than you realize." Kendra gave the woman a hug and continued being led away by her husband.

In the car Blake asked, "What do you mean it helped you being here? What helped you?"

"That was Dad's funeral. I know it sounds strange, but it was. Did you notice how that neighbor sounded like Mom? How the family talked about him being involved, being a quiet man who just took care of things? It seems to me he was a common, everyday man who served in the military, felt it his duty probably. He was obviously deeply loved by friends and family; it's good to know he will be missed. That was Dad, or it could have been. I feel so much lighter suddenly. Strange. Maybe after all this time, God finally granted me closure. I wasn't aware I had even asked for it though, you know what they say, be careful what you ask for, you might get it? I never would have asked for closure in this way. Then again, this is the circle of life, isn't it?"

They continued in the procession of cars back toward home in silence, both dealing with the woes of the tragedy in their own ways. Realizing it was Saturday and it was Cole's birthday, Kendra called Janie to see how the party was going.

"Hello? Mom?" Janie answered, sounding breathless.

"Yeah, you must be having fun; you sound out of breath and winded."

"Gwyn and I are taking Shay to the hospital. They were playing around, and she fell. I think she broke her arm. Sandy is here with everyone else, and she said she'd take care of everything. How far away are you? Will you be home soon? How's Blake?"

"Shay broke her arm?" Kendra repeated.

"What? How did that happen?" Blake jumped in.

Kendra held up her hand to shush Blake. While she continued listening to Janie, the tears began once again to roll down her face. Blake brought the car to a stop alongside the road and waited for Kendra to hang up the phone, relay all the information to him, and then just grabbed her and held her close. He whispered in her ear, "It's okay. You can cry. You've been through a lot. I'm here."

And Kendra cried.

She cried for the people who had lost their lives in that terrible crash. She cried for the loss of her dad. She cried for her granddaughter with possibly a broken arm, and she cried for her mom, feeling the full impact that she was dying, and too soon she would be gone.

CHAPTER 6

The days following her diagnoses would have been considered uneventful to most, but not to Kathleen. She filled her days with caring for others as much as possible. Each morning she started with her two cats, the dog down the way, the people around her, and the friends who stopped by. She was thankful for having a steady influx of people stopping by, checking on her, caring for her as well. With all the activity, though, at the end of each day she would talk to her departed husband, pray to her heavenly Father, and prepare for yet another day of what she considered almost living.

She knew time was passing too quickly. More and more often she was losing her step. Her equilibrium was off slightly, and she was beginning to fall to her left far too frequently. She had decorated her apartment in a crowded manner knowing that someday she would need periodic holdings to maintain her balance. She suspected her daughter, Kendra, knew what she was up to; she just couldn't confirm, and she refused to bring up the subject for open discussion.

Occasionally her sisters and sister-in-law would call to check on her. As welcome as the phone calls were, they were just as aggravating. It was as if nobody believed her. That had been her trouble her entire life—nobody believed her. They didn't believe her when her first husband kidnapped her girls, and they didn't believe when her second husband had beat her senseless during a pregnancy. Of course, in those days, nobody believed the women. She remembered sitting in the courtroom trying to get a divorce from her second husband; she had a new shiny black eye and busted lip to show off as proof to the judge. It wasn't enough though. The judge sat there and had the audacity to ask her what she had done to deserve her husband's retribution.

Being the oldest of eight children had left her bruised and beaten frequently. She may be tiny at only five feet two inches, but she was tough. Life had taught her in the School of Hard Knocks. Beaten if she interfered with her siblings and beaten if she didn't. Beaten by a husband old enough to be her father and beaten by a man that spent more time on the road than at home. Trying to escape one form of getting beat, she often landed in yet another. That was her life—going between the frying pan and the fire.

Then along came Glenn, the only man who had understood and felt the same pain as her. Glenn was the father of six children himself. Two of which he couldn't be sure were his. He was a quiet, hard-working man who wanted nothing more than a loving wife, a good home, good fishing and hunting areas, and a nice place to camp once in a while. Kathleen had been lucky to find him, or lucky that he found her, whichever was the case. Regardless, she knew that God had put them together, and for this, she would be eternally grateful to her loving Father in heaven.

Believing she had stumbled her way through raising her children, she felt the Lord had blessed her for her efforts. He blessed her with a love for all animals and a nature that established trust between her and them almost instantly. She loved being able to pet the raccoons and feed the deer while camping in the fall. She may not have been the best mother or the best wife, but she tried; she had given it all she had, all she was. She tried to provide three meals a day, keep clean clothes in their dresser drawers, and a clean house for them to relax and recuperate from the day. She was doing quite well until she had buried a daughter a few years before, her second one in life. *A mother shouldn't live long enough to bury her children*, she thought. It was time for her to go, and she would welcome the moment. Until then, she would continue using the few gifts God had given her to make others as comfortable as possible while she had the energy to do so.

Things were becoming confused in her mind as of late. It seemed lately she spent more time in the past than in the present, but she couldn't be sure. It had already been over fourteen months since her diagnosis; if they were close, that gave her maybe two more years at best. She was having difficulty hiding her pain from her only child who lived near: her daughter Daphne. Every Monday, like clockwork, Daphne would arrange some activity for them to do together. She didn't mind going to her daughter's home in the mountains; that was her favorite activity of all. With it came a visit to her daughter's store. She enjoyed the employees there, made jokes with them, and generally would do her best to make them laugh. Sometimes it was at her daughter's expense, and for that she was sorry—not sorry enough to stop, though, because it really was funny, and she felt it was important for employees to see their bosses as human and not just a task-issuing machine.

It was cooler in the mountains than in the valley of Phoenix. She loved spending time with the animals at her daughter's ranch, the one she had named "Big Ranch Wannabe." Even though she wished the dogs were better behaved, she still loved that they were always excited to see her, lick her, sit on her, and just love her. Each time the dogs demonstrated their love and excitement, Kathleen would wonder why people couldn't be as loving and forgiving. These dogs were happy to see her whether she remembered to bring them a treat or not. They never ignored her because she had forgotten a treat the last visit. No, they didn't hang onto weaknesses and frailties of the human mind as if they were personal vindictive actions against them. They were spirited, loving, and everything Kathleen wished she could be each and every day. Life would be so much easier if people could be as pleased and excited so easily and just let go of all the burdens of yesteryear.

Daphne was still not willing to admit that her mother was dying. Kathleen could see it in her eyes and hear it in her voice. She was in denial. Even so, she was willing to spend time with her. Her elder daughter, Toni, was supposed to come visit but hadn't. She didn't know why and had heard nothing from her in months. Perhaps it was because having cancer was too close a memory for her. A few years before, Toni had undergone a double mastectomy. Even though everything had gone well, having to face the big C with her mother was probably just too much to handle so soon.

Dannielle had not called or spoken with her in years. She supposed it was because she was closer to the stepmother who raised her. She heard the other children talk about Dannielle being just like her; she had personally never been invited to witness it herself. This daughter had been lost since she was a mere baby thanks to the no-good man who had kidnapped her—like he had a right. God forgive her for the thoughts that went through her mind about that man. Lord knew she was no saint, and she knew she should forgive. It just wasn't there yet.

Her eldest son had nothing to say to her anymore. Their phone calls were short and often one-sided. Kathleen figured he would never forgive her for being such a rotten mother. Although she couldn't, or wouldn't, name specifically what made her so rotten in his eyes, she felt that she had let him down and failed him miserably. Perhaps the good Lord would make up in his life what she had lacked to provide.

Her son Mathew had lived in Phoenix for many years, only recently moving back to Michigan. He had been close to Glenn as well, and although he had tried, he could not stay around her with the memory attached there. He had been her neediest child. She had given and given until there was just nothing left to give. Although she felt bad because she truly wanted to help him, she could see that he would never grow if she continued to provide. He had rushed in after Glenn's death and dispersed all the personal property that could have been her memory. Perhaps it was a good thing. At the time, though, she felt as if he was just one more man in her life taking charge and putting her in her place, failing to recognize the strength that lay within her. That strength which would become her only legacy to her children.

Her youngest son, Ronald, she had lost years ago as well when he had married and converted to that so-called church of his. They had tried over the years to ignore the religious differences without much success. In her mind, that woman he married had corrupted him and convinced him to join that cult of Jehovah's Witnesses.

Kendra had tried repeatedly to assuage her grief concerning his beliefs. At one time, Ronald had rejected the concept of a heavenly beginning and instead adopted the idiotic belief that people came from apes. Even so, despite the religious difference, Ronald was her baby. He was her little womanizer. What a girl pleaser he had been. Through it all, he was her baby boy. There was that part deep down inside him that only a mother could have, and she had it. There was no doubt there was love between them that would continue on long beyond her mortal existence.

Her niece, Lisa, had come as promised, and she had enjoyed that visit immensely. They had become quite close with the deaths that affected them both. Over the past few years, Lisa had lost both her mother and her only sister. Now it was just her and her son that remained of that once strong-willed family of women. Several years ago, when Kathleen's daughter Jo had died, Lisa was there to provide support not only to her but to her cousins as well. Kathleen reflected on how strong Lisa had become and wondered if it was a trait of the family or an individual decision. When Lisa left, they said their final good-byes. It was good.

As for Kendra, she remained distant but efficient. Everything was in order, all the paperwork done, the lists made of what went to whom. And in a way only Kendra could have managed there was only one remaining item that had been brought to her attention. Her spiritual state was not settled. Kathleen was a member of the Church of Jesus Christ of Latter Day Saints and wanted more than anything to attend the Temple in Mesa and be sealed to her husband before she died. More than once Kathleen had attempted to get commitment from Kendra to do the work for her after her death. Kendra had refused. That, too, was yet another blessing.

Over the past few months Kendra had called several times to check point on her progress with what was called a temple recommend. In her church, one had to be considered worthy to attend the temple. The worthiness was determined based on the self-discipline one had to enforce to be obedient to the gospel. While some members of the family thought it too stringent, it was in alignment with many different affiliations. They were basic items: recognizing the Lord Jesus Christ as your Savior; recognizing and accepting His prophets; treating your body as a temple; just to state a few.

Kathleen wasn't sure they would ever let her into the temple because aside from being too stupid in her opinion, she just couldn't seem to stop her judgmental thoughts and condemnations for her ex-husbands and others. If she could get this one thing accomplished, though, she could leave this world being sealed to her husband, and Kendra, in turn, would be sealed to them. This would seal generations together, and she could truly leave in peace.

Her religious belief was a topic that was not openly discussed with the rest of the family. They didn't, or wouldn't, understand. Kathleen reflected on her family and the many denominations of religious beliefs it contained. She had always encouraged her family to be independent and to have faith. Feeling her spiritual duty of a parent was to teach her children about God, Jesus, and the divine nature of our being, she had raised them all Catholic after investigating many churches. When Kendra had introduced her to the Church of Jesus Christ of Latter Day Saints, commonly known as the Mormon Church, she knew that was where she needed to be and she converted.

Only one son refused to acknowledge his divine nature and was a self-proclaimed agnostic. All her other children were Catholic, Jehovah's Witnesses, nondenominational, and Protestant. As a result, she had continued to attend all sorts of churches throughout her life, all of which offered faith and belief in Jesus. All left her with an empty feeling with the exception of the Church of Jesus Christ of Latter Day Saints. She knew you weren't supposed to refer to them as Mormon, but with her memory going, she felt lucky to remember that much of the name. That was the church that had spoken to her soul and was therefore closest to her heart. While her husband had never become a member, she knew that he appreciated the missionaries and the message they shared.

Regardless of his membership, she wanted to be sealed to him. She knew that it would ultimately be his choice to accept any work done vicariously in his name, and she was confident he would want to spend eternity with her. Their love had not disappeared with his death but had strengthened—a fact she could not and would not attempt to explain; it was just the feeling she had within.

Suddenly there came a noise from outside, bringing Kathleen out of her reverie. "Charles, is that you?" Kathleen asked as she walked outside toward the end of her sidewalk. She was certain she had heard something, a rather loud noise, as if someone had fallen.

Charles was her next-door neighbor. He was in his later years, as were all the tenants of the apartment complex. Charles had not lived next door long, and he wasn't quite as old as most tenants; he was, however, an alcoholic. Thankfully, he was not a violent alcoholic, just sloppy and careless. Kathleen had helped him several times in the past as he had staggered home. It was amazing that he had not been in an automobile accident considering how often he returned home late under the influence.

Charles had never confided in Kathleen why he drank so much. He did not talk about his life or any family when he was sober. In fact, he kept to himself. The walls were rather thin despite being made of brick, and she could hear many nights that his television would be louder than it should be. Walking past his picture-frame window, she would see him asleep in his chair. She could tell his life was not a good one, nor did he seem happy at any given moment. With luck, she could occasionally bring laughter to his otherwise solemn disposition. Normally, that would take a lot of effort, and lately she was just running out of energy too early in the evening.

Tentatively, she walked to his door. The screen was closed, but the hardwood door was standing wide open. Charles was facedown on the carpet just inside; it appeared that his foot kicked over the end table on his way down so that it was laying in a manner that would not have permitted the door to close even if it had been on springs.

"Good grief, Charles; are you okay?" she asked as she let herself in to shake him or roll him over. Having served in various nursing situations throughout her life and raising her children along with too many foster children to count, there was little that surprised her anymore. "Lord, help me if I have to move him!" she prayed aloud.

Charles was not a small man. He must have weighed over two hundred pounds and well over a foot taller than Kathleen. She was already picturing in her mind how she might move him if necessary. It would create significant pain in her back, but she would do whatever the Lord wanted done to care for this man.

He had not come to see her since her diagnosis. She figured it made him uncomfortable. For this reason, every time they had passed in the parking lot, she did her best to hide any pain and act young and spry to put his fears at bay. He may not be happy to see her now; although, he also may not remember seeing her. Either way didn't matter to her; she would make sure he was safe for the night.

As she suspected, he had vomited and was lying facedown in it. He could easily drown if she left him like that. It was obvious that he had passed out from his current level of alcohol intake and the fumes coming from his body were enough to inebriate her. Methodically, she went about rolling him over, cleaning his face, securely wrapping her arms under his from behind, and dragging him to the bathroom to start a shower. If she could just wake him enough that he could get himself cleaned up and in bed, her mission would be accomplished. By the grace of God, Charles had a handheld shower device, and she was able to use it to rouse him without having to put him in the shower itself.

Almost two hours later Kathleen was finally heading home to clean herself and take her pain medication. She could hear her phone ringing and could not imagine who would be calling this time of the evening. Upon glancing at her watch, she saw it was nearly 11:00 p.m. *Charles must have started early today,* she thought. *Normally he doesn't show up until well after 2:00 a.m.* Getting inside her own home in time to answer the phone, she chose to ignore it and instead headed for the kitchen cupboard that contained her pills.

After allowing them to slide down her throat, she poured herself another full cup of ice water and made her way into the living room where she sat in her favorite rocking chair just inside the door. She took in a deep breath, let it out slowly, and reached for the telephone.

Beep, the voice message started. "Mom, you there? Just checking to see how you're doing. I know it's late but wanted to know if you had heard from Jerry. He told me he was heading your direction soon for Thanksgiving. Didn't know if you were aware or what your plans were. Oh, well, if you get this anytime soon, feel free to call me back. I'll be up for another half hour or so. Love you."

Jarrod, nicknamed Jerry, was Kendra's youngest son and one of many grandchildren to Kathleen. He had been close to his grandpa, so close, in fact, that he had been the recipient of his grandfather's cherished camper trailer. Kendra said he would "camp" in the driveway each day after school and would have lived there had she allowed it. Perhaps it was because his grandfather was the only father figure in his life, perhaps it was to avoid his sisters that fought constantly, or perhaps it was because he was a quiet, spiritual boy who was much like his grandpa. Whatever the reason, Kathleen knew the camper had gone to the right person—someone who truly appreciated all the hard work Glenn had put into fixing it up. Thinking about that brought a smile to her heart and eased the pain in her back slightly.

Recently, Jerry had returned from his mission in South America. He was a perfect example of a dedicated Latter Day Saint in her opinion, even if he thought he was the furthest thing from ideal. According to Kendra, that was the way it always was with people who were good examples; they always felt they didn't quite measure up to the appropriate standards. She said it had something to do with sufficient humility that made them so ideal. Doing a quick mental assessment of her own inadequacies, Kathleen was not sure she agreed with her baby girl on that matter. Humility, in her own opinion, was where God put you when you got too big for your britches, and Jerry was never too big for his.

"Yes, he called me earlier today." Kathleen answered to no one except her calico cat, Callie. "He said he was going through Albuquerque first to see his grandfather from his dad's side of the family first. Then he was coming here to visit a few days and then home again. At least I get to meet his wife. I understand she's perfect for him, the good little Molly Mormon, only her name is Melissa not Molly. What do you think, Callie, should I call her back? No? I didn't think so. Although, I do hope nothing is wrong. My goodness; it's got to be 1:00 a.m. there; doesn't she ever sleep? Callie, what am I going to do with these kids of mine? You'd think they were raised in a barn with no rules or discipline. Well, I tried. Lord knows I tried."

Kathleen carried on her conversation with Callie while brushing her with a hairbrush that had become a favorite for the cat. It was nice to hear Kendra's voice even if she pretended there was nothing on her mind. Kathleen stretched slightly in her chair. Her back was aching and throbbing from having moved Charles. She tried to relax by sitting back, taking in deep breaths, hoping it would help ease the pain. It did not.

That night, as was her ritual, she sat on her front porch swing. It had begun to rain—a light rain, more than a drizzle but less than a downpour, nothing threatening, which would happen frequently in the valley of Phoenix. She leaned forward, putting her elbows on her knees, clasping her hands together; she peered out at the rain falling into the hedges, and she prayed.

"Oh, honey, I miss you," Kathleen said to her belated husband. "It's so hard to go on alone. Life isn't the same without you here. I wish I could feel your hand in mine again or hear you grunt that dinner was good. Cooking isn't the same when I have to cook for one. Tomorrow I was thinking I could get some groceries and make a big dinner like everyone was still at home. I could take some to Charles and Phyllis or maybe that little old lady around the corner. I never can remember her name. There's nothing to her—reminds me of Jerry. I wonder if she ever eats or even has food to eat. Honey, if you have any power there to ease this pain in my back, please do. And whatever influence you might have, please don't let me lose my sight before I die. I can't imagine not being able to see the beauty of this world while dealing with this pain. I've noticed there's a lump now beside my right eye, and sometimes that side of things gets dark and shadowy. I don't mind the cancer so much. I know it will just bring me to you faster. I am afraid of not seeing though. Lord Jesus, if you would have mercy on me one more time and remove that fear, I will be strong for the rest. I love you, Glenn. I'll see you soon. Good night." And with a small comfort in her heart, she went back inside, leaving the door ajar for the cats to go in and out. Crawling into her bed, she lay down to sleep one more time.

When she awoke the next morning, Kathleen murmured her usual prayer: "Dear Lord Jesus, help me make it through this day." Slowly she threw her legs over the edge of the bed, sat up, petted Callie and her other feline friend, Missy. "What do you think kitties, is today going to be a good day? You hungry? Have you been sitting here just waiting for me to get up and get you some milk? Well, give me a minute; I'm not so young anymore. I'll get you some food." She reached for her glass of water and her pain medication before continuing to stand. *Maybe*, she thought, *if I can head off the pain before it gets too bad I can keep it under control today. Maybe.*

"Mmmm—yellow," Kathleen managed to say into the phone when it jolted her from her nap.

"Mom? Were you sleeping?" Kendra asked. "It's almost noon your time. I tried to wait because I have no idea when you normally get up in the morning."

"Oh, no, honey, I wasn't sleeping, just sitting here watching a little television. What are you doing today? Aren't you at work?"

"Yes, I'm at work. How are you feeling today?"

"I'm fine. Phyllis and I are going to the grocery store later this afternoon, and I thought I might cook a pot roast and share it with her. Lord only knows the last time that woman ate a healthy meal. It was probably the last time I cooked for her." Kathleen reached for her remote control to turn the volume down on the television. "I've got a couple loads of laundry to do, and I need to wash some dishes. Katie came by to borrow my car again; you remember her, don't you? I just don't know, Kendra; sometimes I wonder what God has left for me to do and why he doesn't just take me now."

"Mom, you know what's left for you to do. And since you brought it up, how is that recommend coming along?"

"Oh it's going, it's going. You know, I thought your sister was coming down today, seeing as it's Monday, but I haven't heard from her. Did you hear me, Kendra?" Kathleen asked. She knew that Kendra wasn't listening. It was always obvious when Kendra was working or distracted. Kathleen could hear it in her tone of voice. Not that Kendra ever believed her when she had pointed that out in the past. At least she didn't rush her off the phone like her sister did most days. Kathleen could only hope that part of what she said would get through Kendra's subconscious. She knew her days were no longer exciting to her children; they were barely worth looking forward to herself.

They were nothing like the days when she was up at dawn cooking breakfast for a full house, doing laundry all day, cleaning the house, baking cookies for after school, doing the mending, and so on. Those days were long past. Now, she had this unfilled need to take care of people, only there was no one left to care for—they were all on their own—except for her neighbors occasionally, but even that was challenging with her losing balance, losing her mind, and, essentially, losing her life.

"I'm sorry, Mom, I have to go. I'll call you later in the week, okay? Love you." And with that, Kendra hung up. *Well, almost not like her sister*, Kathleen thought as she went about what her daughter felt was a not-so-worthwhile day of menial tasks and labors.

CHAPTER 7

It was a quiet morning. There were no traffic sounds. There were not even any birds making sounds. The planes that were normally heard periodically off in the distance were also quiet. The only sound was the breeze rustling the leaves above Kendra's head. A cat meowed so softly, she wasn't sure she had really heard it. She didn't bother to look. She was sitting outside at her patio table that was strategically placed between two Texas ash trees. With her feet propped up in a nearby chair, Kendra held her warm cup of herbal tea between both hands, laid her head back against the top of the chair, closed her eyes, and just breathed. *This is what life is about*, she thought. She knew there were people who would be extremely uncomfortable in this silence. Those were the people who needed the sounds of the city—the hustle and bustle of traffic, horns honking, tires screeching, people moving—these were not the sounds that brought peace to Kendra's soul. And this silence, this breeze, this serenity would not bring peace to theirs.

"Whatcha doin'?" Blake asked as he sat down across from her with his own cup of tea.

"Enjoying the silence. Are the kids still sleeping?"

"No, Shay is up. She's watching television. Did Janie say anything else to you?"

"No, I don't really care, I suppose. I just don't understand. Those kids are wonderful. They're smart. Do you think she believes they're too young to pick up on anything she does? Doesn't she realize how much she herself has picked up from my troubled past? I just don't think there's anything we can do really; just be here for them, provide for them. You know?"

"I think she's selfish, but that's just me. Those kids are extremely brilliant. She's not pulling anything off on them. Did you hear that she's leaving them in Dallas with Darren's girlfriend while she goes to Phoenix to see your mom for Thanksgiving? If I understood correctly, his mother will be there visiting his daughter and wanted to see these grandchildren as well."

Darren was Shay's biological father. He had found Janie recently on Facebook and they had reconnected. Even though they had not seen each other much in over nine years, they acted like they had never been apart. What was more frustrating for Kendra was that she felt Janie had immediately and unquestionably assumed her role as the obedient wife once again turning over the main role as parent to a man her children did not know. It didn't matter that he had a pregnant girlfriend and a daughter he was still living with.

"I heard. I don't understand. Why doesn't she let Mom see them one more time? Because Darren's mother has never met them? Well, she isn't dying, is she? I'm not going there." Kendra took in a deep breath and slowly let it out. "Darren could be good for them. I just can't believe she's let him back in her life this way. I know he's

Shay's dad and all, but still. He's a complete stranger to those kids. Doesn't she get that? Do you think if I had told her about Mom sooner it would be any different?"

"No. Yes, you should have told her, maybe. But the fact is you didn't, so why relive it? At any time she could have called your mom and found out herself. Is it your fault she hasn't talked with her grandmother in, what did she say, two or three years?"

"Two."

Waving her word aside as an unimportant fact, Blake continued. "Besides, if your mom wanted her to know, she could have called her as well. This isn't all your responsibility, you know. You are not the official communication channel between your kids and your parents."

They sat in silence for a moment, Kendra pondering what Blake had said.

Kendra knew he was right. He was watching her again with what she called his watchful eye. He was worried about her again, she could tell. *I'm fine, dear; please don't look at me that way and make me feel weak.*

Janie had been living there for almost eight months now and still refused to take on the responsibilities of being a mother. Although she had worked a regular forty hours-plus each week, she had saved nothing. In fact, she was still scraping by.

Blake had confided in Kendra recently that he suspected Janie was doing something with her money but couldn't figure out what exactly. He refused to interfere at this point, but he was watching and paying attention. As long as they lived there, he felt he had some say over those children. Kendra knew that was tenuous ground. While she agreed with him on some levels, she was fearful that her daughter would object and disappear again. Satan had a good hold on her daughter, and he was making his way into those innocent children's lives. What else could she do but pray?

What hurt Kendra the most was that they had both tried extensively to change Janie's life. They had tried to build her self-esteem and help her get on a different road. They had purchased an enrollment in one of those online dating services so she could see the variation of men that might be interested in her and not be limited to just those abusive, welfare-minded idiots she often took up with. They had encouraged her to begin college, learn a trade, any trade. Janie said she was interested in cooking, so they helped gather information with the local culinary schools. She said she was interested in nursing, so Blake had obtained information from his coworkers on the myriad of medical avenues that could provide her with self-worth and independence.

Janie had played along, acting as the grateful daughter the entire time. Now it seemed she had only been taking advantage of the situation. Right now, Kendra felt her only stability was Blake and the Lord, the only men she could count on, believe in, and trust. Often she had relied on her faith, and she had never been disappointed, God had always been there to carry her when times were rough. Blake was there to love her, hold her and believe in her. She hadn't realized how much she had needed him until he appeared. She hadn't even realized how much she had been praying for him until he confided in her his own prayers. If He needed her to be strong for Blake, for Janie, for her grandchildren, or for her Mother, then she could. She could do anything He gave her because she knew she wouldn't be doing it alone.

Their silent camaraderie was suddenly interrupted when Janie came pulling into the driveway driving her beat-up, used, navy blue Cadillac which she had marketed as being in pretty good shape. The story behind the purchase always left Kendra exhausted. She couldn't understand why Janie felt the need to justify the purchase. It was her money and her life. Nothing else had seemed to matter; why the car did, she didn't know.

"Are the kids up?" Janie asked as she stepped out of the car, still dressed in her work clothes. Her tone was harsh, brief, and direct. She glared over at Kendra, waiting for an answer.

"Good morning to you too," Kendra replied casually. Although she appeared calm and indifferent on the outside, her heart was beating so loudly in her own ears she was afraid she wouldn't know if someone spoke.

"Are they up?" Janie repeated.

"Why don't you go in the house and see for yourself?" Blake interjected, ending the shadowed altercation.

"It's going to be another beautiful day, dear." Kendra smiled at her husband as she made her way to follow Janie into the house.

"Grandma! Did you know we're going to Dallas today to visit my dad and his family? His mom is going to be there. She's coming all the way from North Carolina to meet us!" Shay wrapped her arms around Kendra's waist, giving her a big hug.

"Yes, honey, I know." Kendra was half hugging her back, half stroking her long, blond hair. Blake had walked up right behind her and, being the typical grandfather, could not allow for such a sentimental moment. Kendra needed to smile, and the grandkids needed to see her smile as much as he did. With one hand reaching to catch Shay, his other hand sneaked up behind Kendra, grabbing her from behind to spin her around and plant a big kiss on her neck, making her squeal and squirm and lose her cup onto the carpeted flooring.

With the mood reset from melancholy to laughter, Blake had successfully relieved some of the growing tension between Janie and Kendra. This was one of the many reasons Kendra loved him and appreciated the fact he knew her so well. Janie and Kendra continued to curtly ignore each other while making fun and playing games with the kids. As they were saying good-bye, Kendra's other daughter, Jenny, was calling from Japan. It was a relief because Kendra hated good-byes. At every good-bye she could remember as a child, her mother would cry, her dad would mumble and turn away, and she would be left with a feeling of guilt. She mostly felt guilty for not having the feeling to cry as well or even feel sad that someone was leaving. In her mind, a good-bye was just a "see you later," so there was no reason to get all emotional about it.

Jenny was in the navy and currently serving in Japan. She had been dealing with medical issues periodically throughout the year, and Kendra was worried this phone call was yet another medical problem. It wasn't; Jenny was just excited about finally getting orders for Texas, bringing her closer to home. She wouldn't be there until the following summer because she would be doing a short stay in San Diego upon arriving stateside again.

She was receiving some additional training in her field before her permanent assignment.

With the house empty again of extra bodies, it was a quiet Thanksgiving spent in Brummley at Blake's work as usual. Kendra took real pleasure in helping to prepare a Thanksgiving feast for those on duty instead of spending time with their families. It didn't bother her that Blake always worked. Usually it was just the two of them, and she could just as easily be with him at work as home. By being with him at work, it allowed someone else to be home with his family. Not that she was a good cook; she wasn't. She would make a salad of some kind, and the crew would make a wonderful dinner.

Her mother, on the other hand, would go all out; she loved to cook for a crowd, and she loved the holidays—all of them. Although there were several phone calls back and forth to Phoenix, it seemed everyone was getting along there. Kathleen had cooked what was described as a huge dinner, enough to feed a small army. They had spent the day at Daphne's Big Ranch Wannabe and her store. They watched movies and visited; she heard Melissa had even sung a song for them. She had a beautiful voice, and Kendra was certain that everyone had enjoyed it. While it brought a sense of peace to Kendra knowing they were spending time together, getting to know each other again as adults, there was still a small, still voice in her mind, or perhaps her soul, somewhere telling her to watch out; it was coming. She just refused to acknowledge whatever "it" could be.

As Christmas approached, the tension continued to build. Darren and Janie wanted to give the children a video game system for Christmas, and Kendra was getting more and more upset. Finally, while on the phone on her drive to work one morning, she let Darren have it with both barrels.

"What is wrong with you two? Do you really think these kids need a game? A game? Don't you think they would much rather have a bedroom of their own maybe? Maybe, just maybe, they would like a home that was theirs instead of a bedroom the entire family shared in my home. Or wait, maybe they would like to have clothes that actually fit them and were clean and not stained. Or maybe they might like to have time with their parents in a place just for them. Oh, I'm sorry, neither you nor Janie can provide those things, right? You want to provide the superficial things like games so that they stayed glued to a television screen instead of using the wonderful minds that God gave them! I keep forgetting that your generation feels they don't have to use their mind, just their thumbs. Man, it is a good thing that God gave you thumbs to differentiate you from the apes!"

"You know what, Kendra? I thought maybe you would be on my side. You know how hard I worked to find her and have my daughter back, and if I could afford it right now, they would have their own home. Janie and I are just not ready for that yet."

"You're not ready? Why am I not surprised? You weren't ready to marry my daughter, when you did. You weren't ready to have children when you did. You weren't ready to leave North Carolina when Janie left, and truth be told, you're just not ready to leave your girlfriend. Instead, you're setting an example for these children that is unacceptable. You should be teaching them things like loyalty and dedication and integrity. Instead you teach

Cole it's okay to have two women, and you teach those girls that it's okay to share your man with other women. What kind of example is that? Of course, you would have to first possess integrity and loyalty in order to teach it to those kids!" Kendra wanted to reach through the phone and slap him as hard as she could. She knew she should shut up; she just couldn't. Darren had moved in with her about four months after his marriage to Janie; by then Janie had already run off with Ty. After almost a year it was apparent that Janie was not coming back and Kendra forced Darren to move on with his life. She had lost contact with him shortly after he moved out. It was a strange relationship. She didn't know Darren, but he was her son-in-law. The more she tried to help him, the more her daughter avoided her. There was no winning amongst all this drama. She was exasperated.

"You're right, Kendra; you're always right. I'll take care of it, and the kids will have their own place. At the same time you are not going to tell me what I can and can't give my children for Christmas. I'll get them whatever I want." Darren's voice was rising and becoming more hostile. It was obvious he was losing the battle to maintain control.

"Whatever, Darren, I don't have time for this. Get them whatever you want, but they will not connect some game system to my televisions. Understood?" She was finished and almost to work. She needed to take a few minutes to regroup before entering her office, and if she didn't get off the phone, she wouldn't have those few minutes.

"You know where you can go, Kendra. I don't have to say it. Good-bye." And with that, Darren hung up.

Before she could even toss the phone onto the passenger seat, her message sound went off.

"Whatcha doin'?" Kendra received on her cell phone. Her friend, Sandy, often would text her this message during the day. "Can u talk?"

"Working and yes," Kendra text back, her phone ringing immediately after pressing send.

"Hey, what's up?" Kendra asked. She was tired and welcomed the interruption.

"I'm in town, thought you might want to have coffee," Sandy responded.

"I can't. I have a meeting in about fifteen minutes. I cannot wait for this week to end though. Blake and I are leaving Friday morning for Florida. I *so* need this week off!"

Blake had arranged for them to have a condo for a week in Florida. Normally, they would try to go to Disney World, but not this year. They really wanted to take the grandchildren but were not allowed to, which was no great surprise.

"I had another fight with Darren this morning on my way in. I just don't understand them. You met him; what do you think? Am I crazy? Am I being to overbearing or controlling?"

"No! Kendra, those kids and your daughter live in your house; that alone gives you the right. Those are your grandkids. I met Darren's girlfriend too, remember? She seemed just as nuts as Darren and Janie. I'm sorry. I know I shouldn't say anything because she is your daughter, but, Kendra, she uses you all the time. You don't have to put up with that. I know you're tired and stressed, that's all. Who wouldn't be? You're dealing with her and your mom and your sister, give yourself a break already. I mean really, sometimes I get so tired I can't remember what it is I'm supposed to be thinking. I can only imagine what you're going through."

Kendra knew what Sandy said was true. At least, she knew her friend was giving her the validation she needed to the nagging questions in the back of her mind, *am I being controlling? Is it really my right to give my opinion?*

"Thanks, Sandy. I appreciate you, you know? Now go earn your free car with all those parties you're going to book," Kendra replied in a lighter tone, gently reminding Sandy they should be focused on something positive and not all the drama that followed Janie.

"Yeah, I could say the same to you, too. Have a good day. See ya laters."

"Ciao, bella!"

"Whatever, freak!" Sandy disconnected the conversation, leaving Kendra laughing her way into a nearby parking spot.

Kendra did not find the peace at the beach she had hoped to find. She had tried and had even had a few good evenings there. She just couldn't relax. In fact, she found more enjoyment walking the beach for hours than in watching the sun set over the water.

Having endured the trip, Kendra couldn't wait to get home again, back to her ground, where she was in control and could easily move from one topic or task to the next in order to feel productive.

As they pulled into the drive, she saw the house was dark. There were no other cars in the driveway. She could feel her adrenaline rising. She knew she would not like whatever it was she was about to encounter. As she entered the front door and reached for the light switch, Kendra could feel the emptiness. It was too quiet. Even the animals were quiet. She walked to the bedroom where the kids slept and turned on the light. Slowly she turned around and walked back into the kitchen just as Blake was entering from the garage.

"What's wrong?" Blake asked. "Are you okay? You look pale."

"They're gone," Kendra replied as she dug her cell phone out of her purse to call Janie.

"Hello?" Janie's voice sounded as if she didn't have a care in the world.

"Hey, we just got home. Noticed you moved out. You weren't going to say anything? No note, no nothing?" Kendra was trying to be calm but was not hiding her anger very well at all.

"The horses are fed for the night, dogs and cats taken care of. You and Blake should be able to relax and rest up from your trip. We'll talk later, Mom," Janie said, ignoring her mother's question.

"Janie, I don't want to wait until some other time. Where did you go? Gwyn's?

"Mom, your house was too small for all of us. Don't worry about us; we're fine."

"You're not answering me. What's going on?"

"Bye, Mom." And with that, Janie hung up.

"She hung up on me." Kendra said, turning toward Blake, who was coming out of the bedroom having had to see the proof for himself.

"What do you mean she hung up? Give me the phone." Blake was furious.

"Janie? What are you doing? Do you think your mother deserves this?"

"Tell her I'm done. I'm not doing this again. As far as I'm concerned, I'm dead to her." Kendra said from the sidelines. Her heart was breaking, and she was struggling to hang on to the anger. Darn that friend Sandy; she would never be in tune to this feeling thing if Sandy wouldn't have pointed it out. Now it was apparent what it felt like to have someone hurt your feelings, to have someone break your heart, and to experience that pain without the anger, but with the acceptance that it was their freedom of choice to do so. *This is the last time Janie will do this to me*, she thought. And as if those words triggered a physical action, a door closed in her heart. It was done.

"You don't mean that, Kendra," Blake said, surprise in his tone as he turned toward her, hanging up the phone and setting it on the counter. "Yes. I do. At least the first time she did this I got a phone call. This time, nothing? No warning, no discussion, not even willing to talk to me now? I'm done. First time shame on her, second time shame on me; there won't be a third."

CHAPTER 8

Kendra tried not to act surprised when her mom got out of the car at the airport pick-up area. *She's aged, a lot*, she thought. She had lost weight as well. She looked like she was ninety years old if she were a day. Giving her mom a hug and a kiss on the cheek, Kendra tried to be gentle. Suddenly, this woman who could take on the world seemed fragile. She was glad she decided to come out early and spend a few days with her before going on to her convention. Now, she wondered if she should even go to the convention.

"I'm so glad you came," Phyllis exclaimed as Kendra got in the car. "Your mom can't drive at night anymore, and she doesn't like driving in traffic during the day. You know she's been sick again, right? She always does much better when she knows you're coming."

Kendra simply smiled at Phyllis and turned in her seat to talk with her mom, who had opted to sit in the back.

"How you doin,' Mom?"

"Oh, I'm fine, honey. Don't you listen to Phyllis. She thinks I'm dying if I sneeze. I actually feel pretty good now that I've lost a few pounds."

"Ha! She's lost a few pounds because she's not eating! That's what it is; don't let her fool you," Phyllis interjected.

Kendra felt like she was in a tennis match, first looking at her mom, then Phyllis, then her mom. She didn't know who to believe. She couldn't understand why Daphne had not called or said anything to prepare her for this. There was a difference. *Mom has changed over the past few months. Couldn't Daphne see it?*

The visit went well. There was no tension buildup or hidden frustration. Kendra found herself with more patience when her mom rambled. She watched her closely, watched her movement and saw her stumble on occasion. She also noticed her mom didn't have the energy she usually had. They spent most of the time watching movies and relaxing. Kathleen made her favorite dishes for dinner and had even gone out of her way to purchase tortillas and cheese because she knew Kendra liked Mexican food.

Before going on to the convention, Kathleen asked if Kendra could take Missy in to see the local veterinarian. She had clumps of something all over her back and wouldn't allow Kathleen to get a close look. Only, Kathleen couldn't catch Missy to put in the carrier.

"Why hasn't Daphne helped you?" Kendra inquired, after using almost every part of her body to push the huge cat into a tiny carrier.

"Missy won't go near Daphne; at least she likes you," Kathleen replied.

"Well if she did, she won't now." Kendra laughed.

As they were approaching the parking lot to the veterinarian, Kathleen looked over at Kendra. "Do you think they'll give me a discount if I tell them she's a stray?"

Laughing again, Kendra replied, "Mom, have you looked at your cat? You've got Lucifer from Cinderella in that carrier!"

"They gave me a discount when I brought her here to be spayed; you don't think they would believe me?"

"Mom, no. Especially if they know you own her from bringing her here to be spayed. That cat is too fat for anyone to believe it's a stray."

"I know you think I'm stupid for asking. Money is tight, Kendra, and if I can save a few dollars by saying she's a stray, then I will."

"Would you please stop saying you're stupid? You're not stupid. If money is so tight, Mom, I'll pay for the visit. Okay? Will you let me do that?"

"No, honey. This isn't your responsibility."

Watching her mother throughout the experience only confirmed to Kendra that perhaps she was much worse than she claimed. Kendra shared a knowing wink with the receptionist as her Mom proclaimed the cat to be a stray. When they were called back into a room, Kendra managed to slip away and pay for the visit without her mom's knowledge. The receptionist had played along on the way out by saying Kathleen had a credit that would be applied, and they would send a bill if there was any balance due.

As it turned out, the cat only had some fur balls gathering on its backside that it was unable to reach because it was too fat. While Kendra sat on the floor that evening, grooming the cat as the doctor had instructed,

Kathleen reached down and started playing with her hair, twisting it into various hairstyles.

"Do you want me to do your hair before you leave for your convention tomorrow?" Kathleen asked softly.

Unable to speak, Kendra simply shook her head and laid it upon her mother's lap.

Kendra went on to her convention the next day as planned and struggled to be inspired. Normally, these gatherings were overwhelmingly inspirational. They were filled with training and motivational activities that would keep her fired up until the next convention. The meetings were arranged in various places in the United States and usually held about every quarter to keep the sales force inspired. This time, Kendra just couldn't seem to care. She tried. She tried to get excited about a goal; it's just that the goal never reached her heart, and if it's not in the heart, it's not truly the goal.

At the end of it all, Kendra and a few of her girlfriends drove up to the mountains to have dinner with Daphne. Taking the chance that they would all prefer being with Daphne from now on, Kendra drove the crowd toward her sister's store. As was the case, Daphne wouldn't have her plans interrupted, even if her sister was visiting from out of town. She had planned a date for that evening so instead of cancelling or rescheduling, she brought him along. Kendra was fascinated that Daphne would bring a first date to a dinner with a group of women she had never met before. Either her sister really didn't like this guy, or she was really so wrapped up in herself she couldn't see how uncomfortable it made everyone. And to top it off, the guy was a real jerk, and not just in Kendra's opinion, but all three of her girlfriends' as well.

Kendra could not understand why Daphne would date someone so obnoxious. The only explanation Daphne would provide was that he was the brother of a close friend. *Ah, yes*, Kendra thought, *back to the ole never-burn-a-bridge philosophy*. She shook her head, resigned that she would never understand her sister.

Overall, the evening was a huge success. Even though Daphne's date was a jerk, he was a good sport. One of the ladies used him in a demonstration that had everyone laughing to tears. He started a heated conversation on direct sales and tried repeatedly to give everyone a sales pitch on some investment opportunity. At the end of the evening, Daphne's date obligation was met, all had a great time, new friendships were formed, and Kendra was able to drive back to the hotel in good spirits.

Before going home on Sunday, Kendra went to church with her mom. She met her bishop, his wife, and three children. She had met them before but couldn't remember their names. She thought it was funny that her mom went to church with snacks in her purse for the toddlers and gifts for the older children. The kids considered her "Grandma Kathleen" and adored being with her. Kendra was fascinated watching the interaction. She had never inherited this from her mom; in fact, it would never occur to her to take snacks and goodies to church for the children who sat around her. The bishop could see no reason that Kathleen should not have her temple recommend by her birthday in March. Although Kendra wasn't exactly a planner, the temple trip would require coordinating many schedules.

The short time to Kathleen's birthday flew by. Finally, the day had come to go to the temple in Mesa. Blake, Kendra, Jerry, and Melissa had all showed up for the occasion. As they were all getting ready to leave the small apartment, Kendra was pulled aside by her older sister. Daphne did not understand and was not able to be part of the ceremony. Being a Catholic, she did not have the right permissions to attend any Latter Day Saint Temple ceremony.

"You know, the Catholic Church doesn't have secret ceremonies that family members can't attend. Why does your church?" she asked.

"Daphne, I know you don't understand," Kendra replied. You don't have to. You don't even have to agree with it." Kendra reached over and touched Daphne's arm lightly. "It would be nice though if you would just allow Mom this time." Removing her hand again, she looked her sister in the eye. "If you believe it's a waste of time and not real, fine, so be it, but it's real to her, and that's what matters. Let's assume that everything about the Mormon Church is made up; who is it hurting for Mom to go through with this and be sealed to Dad? Does it hurt you? Does it hurt Dad? No, but it does give Mom a sense of accomplishment, of closure and more importantly of eternal love. Her work will be complete, and she'll be ready to let go."

"Maybe I don't want her to let go," Daphne said.

"Daphne, I think she's hanging on and fighting so she could do this herself. I have told her repeatedly I wouldn't do it for her. I personally believe in this. I'm not asking you to believe and neither is Mom."

While Daphne did not understand, she decided to drop it and allow them their special time in the temple.

It was Kendra's influence that had brought the missionaries to her mom's door and ultimately led to her baptism in the church. This was just an age-old discussion that the family often had—why this religion and not that one. Kendra was tired of it because in her mind everyone had the same gift from God, and that gift was freedom of choice. She really didn't care which religion people chose as long as it didn't cause bodily damage or break laws; as long as there was Christ in their lives, it would all work out.

It was a beautiful day at the temple. The sun was shining; it wasn't too hot nor was it too cold. They comfortably sat outside the temple, allowing Kathleen to catch her breath. She was excited and nervous, which caused her to tire more easily. Jerry and his wife had arranged to be there for the occasion as well. In fact, he not only planned to be there, he had been instrumental in ensuring the proper paperwork was completed and had made arrangements for him to be part of the ceremony as the proxy for Glenn. Blake would be a witness, and everyone would be sealed.

Immediate calm engulfed Kendra as they walked into the Temple. They checked in at the front by showing the proper documentation. Kendra only left her mother's side when the ceremony required it. She watched her mom through the events that followed. She studied her movements, her facial expressions, and even felt the peace that seemed to sink into her mother's heart. The spiritual experience was powerful, and when the sealings were complete, Kendra's fear subsided. She knew she would have her parents for eternity. Watching her mother look into the mirrors, Kendra saw the same in Kathleen, the fear was gone, acceptance had taken its place. Her Mom had closure now, there was no reason for her to linger here on earth. Relaxing back at Kathleen's tiny apartment, everyone was feeling good; they were happy. It was a good visit, and Kathleen had said it was the best birthday she ever had.

On the flight home, Kendra sat beside Blake holding his hand with her head on his shoulder. She played back the events from the temple in her mind. The only disparate feeling Kendra could remember was when she witnessed her mom in the clerk's office establishing the initial paperwork. The question had come up regarding her mom's parents. Kendra heard her mother's voice crack as she stated she did not know who her dad was and asked how could God allow her this when she was too stupid to know a simple thing like her Dad's name? Kendra was surprised at the frustration she witnessed and quickly assured her mom that it was okay; she was not too stupid because God knew who her dad was, and it would all be handled by Him anyway. She had a stepfather who had loved her, and she had a heavenly Father who loved her—that was all that mattered. Grateful for the assurance offered by her daughter, Kathleen once again committed herself to accept the wonderful gifts received in the temple. While Kendra had escorted her from the office, she realized how important this was to her and her mother. Closing her eyes and taking in a deep breath, Kendra did not want to accept the end was near.

While Kathleen had appeared small and weak, she was stronger than Kendra had given her credit for. She persevered through the following days. She had called Kendra to keep her informed about her activities and her health. She attended birthday parties, baby showers, and visited with church members. The only sign that Kathleen was getting weaker was that she had agreed to allow a woman in the ward to do her laundry. Kendra knew how important doing laundry was to her mother and was surprised to hear about the change. Her mom not doing laundry was like a horse not knowing to run. And while she recognized the impact of the change, she was still not prepared for the next phase of her illness.

"Well, I went to the doctor again today," Kathleen said into the phone with a wary voice.

"And?" Kendra inquired, sitting down on her couch, muting the television, and giving her mother undivided attention and focus. She could hear something in the tone but was not willing to give it a name.

"They put me on hospice today, although I don't know why; I feel fine." There was no shock or surprise in Kathleen's voice. There was sadness and a realization that it was getting closer, a realization that still hit Kendra in the solar plexus, causing her to breathe shallowly while she regained her composure.

"Want me to come out?"

"If you want to. Nothing has changed though. They say you can be on hospice for a long time, years even. It's not necessarily going to be the end any time soon. I still have at least a year and a half or so, maybe even as much as two years. You may want to come meet the hospice people though."

Oh, Mom, Kendra thought, *I've never heard anyone being on hospice for years. .*

"I have a website for you; they're Hospice of the Valley, and they are the nicest people you've ever met. You'll never guess what my nurse's name is. It's Kendera! Isn't that funny? She spells it differently; I can't remember right now, but it's pronounced the same. She could be your sister; she would fit right into this family. When would you be thinking about coming out?"

Kendra was trying to process all of the news. She followed the conversation in bullets: hospice, nurse named Kendra, different spelling, when should she go?

"Let me talk with Blake, and I'll call you back. Did you know that Jenny will be stateside soon? She should be in San Diego sometime next month."

"Yes, she called me. She's going to come out here if she can. She's done good with her life, hasn't she? She's a bright girl."

"Yes, she is a bright girl." Kendra swallowed, remembering the words that Kathleen had spoken at the dinner the year before. This was her mom, and what was said a year ago was moot.

"You know your other daughter still owes me money. She ran up my long distance bill when she was here for Thanksgiving, and it cost me $5.17 for her to call that husband of hers."

"Want me to track her down and beat it out of her? Or would you rather I just send you the money?"

"No! I don't want you to beat it out of her. Good God, Kendra, where do you come up with stuff like that?"

There was the mom that Kendra knew so well. That was the right tone and force. She would much rather hear this than the sound of defeat.

"Anyway, smarty pants, I spoke to Jerry the other day as well," Kathleen went on. "He said they were thinking about getting pregnant but didn't think the time was right. I told him the time would never be right."

"Nope, it never is, as we both know."

"Phyllis had her son visit the other day. I guess he just got out of jail on bail. She swears he's a good kid, so I never say anything to her that might hurt her feelings. He's going to use her again though and end up right back there."

"Yep, probably."

"Your sister doesn't think I should be on hospice yet; she blames the doctor. I know I don't eat as much as I used to; it just hurts so much to swallow. They did that procedure, and it still hurts. He said that there's nothing more that can be done."

"I'm sure Daphne's right, Mom. Isn't she always?" *Stop that!* Kendra reprimanded herself. *Why do I always do that? I'm better than that.*

"Well, honey, Katie just walked up with Buddy. How you doin,' little guy? Do you want a treat? I gotta go, call me later, okay? Love you." And she hung up.

Kendra sat on the couch and tried to regroup. She remembered Katy from her earlier visit. She lived a few apartments down from her mother and had the cutest little dog named Buddy. Kendra liked Katy and was glad to have her as another source of information. Looking at the clock, Kendra saw Blake would not be home for hours, which meant she had time to process. She debated calling Daphne and finally decided it might not hurt.

"Hey, sista! Whatcha doin'?" she said in the most energetic voice she could muster.

"Oh, hey, Kendra. I'm glad you called. Did Mom call you?" Daphne sounded as if she might actually have time to talk.

"Yes, I just hung up. I was curious—"

"Can you believe it? I think they put her on hospice because she won't have chemotherapy. Seriously, Kendra, her doctor is a real piece of work. She was just downright nasty to me when I went. She actually said to me, 'I don't know why you're asking so many questions now considering the fact your mother's had cancer for almost two years.'"

"Well, perhaps—"

"Obviously, she doesn't know Mom. Like we're supposed to know when to believe her. You know that Mom's been saying this stuff almost our entire life. How are we supposed to know?"

And to think I felt bad a minute ago for thinking ill of her. It was obvious to Kendra that this really wouldn't be a conversation or dialogue about her mom's condition. Daphne was more in denial than before. Somewhere in the back of Kendra's mind she recognized the fear in Daphne's voice. She pushed it away, refusing to acknowledge it or give it a name, instead relying on old thought patterns of Daphne's self-centered ways.

The one-sided conversation continued for what Kendra thought an exceptionally long time. Daphne had never sounded so scared, so lost. *Is she looking to me for strength?* Unable to get a word in and uneasy with her new thoughts about her sister, Kendra simply listened. It was agreed that she would return to Phoenix soon.

"I love you, little sister, you know that, right?" Daphne said.

"I do know it. I love you too, Daph. See you soon." And Kendra hung up.

When Blake came home that evening, they would talk. In the meantime, she would need to look through her schedule.

Still unbalanced by her conversation with her sister, and with time on her hands until Blake returned, Kendra decided Sandy was just the person she needed to hear.

"Hey, Sandy, whatcha doin'?" Kendra asked, trying to hide the emotion in her tone.

"Nothin.' What're you doing?"

"Mom just called. They put her on hospice." Kendra just blurted it out, like she always did when talking with Sandy. That was the beauty of good friends, something she had missed her entire life by avoiding women. Being able to just blurt out anything without judgment and not only be accepted, but given empathy and understanding in return. It may not be all women, but it was certainly how she viewed Sandy.

"I'm so sorry. You going out there? Is there anything I can do?" Sandy's tone was immediately soft and caring. Kendra could always count on her to be supportive and understanding. Somewhere deep down she felt a twinge of guilt because she knew that she was not this good of a friend to Sandy. It was very one-sided with

Sandy coming out the victor in the best at being a friend competition.

"Yes, I'm going to go. We have that Children's Miracle Network booth to do here soon, so I'll wait until after that. I don't want to leave you hanging, and Mom said it's not an emergency. It's just the beginning of the end I suppose."

"I can cover it if you need me to. I'm here for you for whatever you need."

"It'll most likely be mid- to late June before I make it out there. I have things I need to take care of first. In the meantime, I can call them and get any information. Daphne isn't much help; she's in denial. Mom's neighbor Katie always gives me the worst possible scenario possible. I don't know what to believe. I'm not really sure if waiting is the right thing or if jumping is the right thing."

"I know what you mean. Just pray about it and you'll know. Speaking of not knowing, have you heard from Janie?"

"Who?"

"Kendra, you know who I mean."

"Hmmm, nope, can't recall a Janie. Are you sure I know her?" Kendra's tone was immediately cold and indifferent. *Sandy knows better than to push this button*, Kendra thought; *there goes her best friend award.*

"Okay, so have you heard anything about your grandkids?"

"Oh, sure I have. They're doing good. They've been in North Carolina now since, what, February? They're out there near Darren's parents, and my ex lives out there, so they have plenty of family."

"I thought his family was in Dallas?"

"No, he used to live in Dallas when he was with his girlfriend, but since he left her for Janie, I guess they weren't welcome there anymore. Go figure, seems to be a theme for them."

"Well, I was fixin' to go into town. I need to make some product deliveries and go by Wal-Mart. Want to go?"

"No, but thanks. If you want to come by, though, come on. Oh, and remind me later to tell you about my conversation with Daphne just now. Really weird if you ask me."

"What happened?"

"Not now, you're on your way out," Kendra teased. She knew Sandy couldn't ignore something once it had been said. It was like dangling a shiny object in front of her and asking her to not look.

"What? Tell me, heifer."

"Ah, my favorite pet name. Well, since you put it that way." Kendra laughed. "It's no big deal, really. I think for the first time I saw a side of Daphne I never knew was there. She's scared."

"Well, duh. It's her mom too, you know."

"No. It was more than that. It was like she was the little sister and I was older. It was really weird. Let me think on it some more; maybe a better description will come to me."

"Fine. But do me a favor."

"Sure. What?"

"Stop minimizing what you do, Kendra. You are strong and feeling, and you have your own way of caring for people. It doesn't matter that you don't do it like your mom or like your sister. You take care of people your way, the way God intended you to. So stop acting like it's nothing. It's a gift from God Himself."

"Yes, Mother." Kendra tried to make light of what she knew was heartfelt from her friend. "I'll talk to you later."

"Bye."

Kendra felt better hanging up the phone. It was amazing that Sandy knew how to do that. She could make her laugh at herself and totally distract her with no notice or preparation. She was a good friend.

After confirming with Blake and rearranging her schedule, Kendra was finally on the plane to Phoenix. Not knowing what to expect with this visit, she was unable to prepare. Instead, she immersed herself in her work, being glued to her laptop through the entire flight. Her mom did not pick her up from the airport this time. She was no longer able to drive, Phyllis was unavailable, and it was a very long drive for her sister; she had not wanted to ask. Instead Kendra arranged to take the shuttle.

She didn't think it was possible, but her mom looked older still. *She's disappearing*, Kendra thought. Maybe Daphne didn't notice because she was there all the time; she saw her every week. *We often miss what is right in front of our noses*, she remembered hearing. Kathleen slept more these days, and she kept a daily history of all medications. She would put on gospel music channels, gospel DVDs or even gospel records. Kendra didn't mind gospel; it helped uplift her own spirits.

During the short stay, Nurse Kendera came by, and Kendra learned they were a lot alike. With the exception of an extra *e* in the name, that is. They had a good conversation, and Kendra was comfortable that she would be a good match to care for her mom. The social worker, Elaine, came as well and provided Kendra with a pamphlet of information about the stages of death. Kendra had remembered seeing it when her dad had died, so she had specifically asked for it. She couldn't remember the signs and knew there was information somewhere, which would give her clues that there were months left or weeks, days, or hours. The social worker was very polite, soft spoken, and had a very open personality. Kendra had walked Elaine to her car so she could ask for the pamphlet out of earshot from her mother.

"Thank you so much for the information; it's going to come in handy. It will help me be better prepared and to keep the family informed," Kendra stated.

"Oh, you're welcome," Elaine replied. "Your mother is so sweet; she's just a character. She talks about you all the time. She's very proud of you."

"Hmm," was the only response Kendra supplied with a smile on her face.

"Well, if you need anything, just call."

"Elaine, one more thing, if you don't mind."

"Yes?"

"I live near Austin, it's only about a two-and-a-half-hour flight, but when you schedule that flight for tomorrow or the next day, it's really expensive. If there is anyway possible, please call me when you see the signs. That way I can make the reservations at least ten days ahead of time. I have no problem coming out here to stay, so it doesn't even have to be the last days. Does that make sense?"

"It does. As long as you realize we can only give you our opinion. We don't pretend to be the Omnipotent."

"I know that. I didn't mean it like that, I meant anything at all, if you feel she needs someone here, call me. Okay?" Kendra was struggling to keep her emotions under control. She needed to get in automatic mode to be successful.

"No problem, Kendra; you got it. I'll let Kendera know as well. We'll keep in touch with you and keep you updated of any changes. You take care and have a safe trip home."

"Thank you, Elaine."

"She's very lucky to have you here and that you're willing to take care of her. Many people don't have that." Elaine gave Kendra a hug and proceeded to get in her car.

Over the next few days, hospice arranged for Kathleen to have first alert; in case anything happened while she was alone, she could just push the button on her necklace, and help would be on the way. They arranged for a meal a day to be delivered through the Meals-on-Wheels program. They switched over all her medications and oxygen from insurance to hospice care and replaced her portable oxygen tanks. They visited her regularly and kept progress notes. They were extremely helpful, and Kendra felt better about returning home.

Before leaving, she decided to spend a night with her sister. She felt drawn to Daphne somehow and needed to see her and spend time with her. Daphne had not been around much even though she had called frequently. In reality, it had to be difficult for her sister to manage her store while trying to be involved in her mom's progress. Kathleen could be very challenging at times, and Daphne was a one-woman show. She was the store, and if she could not be available then her business would suffer.

"How are you holding up, Daph?" Kendra sat at the kitchen table, laptop open, her e-mail opened and waiting.

"Busy, busy, you know how it is. Just the other day I had to meet with this vendor, and Mom was calling me; Irene said it sounded important, so I took the call. She was just upset because Katie wanted to borrow her car and she didn't know if she should let her. The woman is driving me crazy. Don't misunderstand, I love her; I just can't pay attention to her 24/7. Know what I mean?" Daphne was tired and emotional. Kendra just watched her, taking in everything—the pitch of her voice, the rise and fall of her emphasis, her body language, her expression. For the first time Kendra was beginning to see the fear in Daphne's eyes. There was more to this relationship between them than she understood. She didn't need to understand it though; she was just grateful that she could recognize the fear and denial so she could adjust accordingly.

Daphne was strong and independent. There was a lot to admire in her. Several years before, when she had had surgery, Kendra had come out to care for her a few days. *Those were the best times*, Kendra thought. Not the surgery part, but the part when Daphne wasn't the personality but the person. Kendra liked her then. She could relate to her and talk with her when she was just the person. Like any other person, Daphne had her fears, her hurts, her dreams, and underlying it all was her loneliness. Kendra had never seen it before. How could Miss Popularity be lonely? Truth of it being she was. Superficial acquaintances did not make up for having a loving, supportive husband to hold, confide in, and find comfort in.

"You know I'm coming out to stay when hospice calls, right?" Kendra tried to offer some assurance.

"I know; I'm so glad you are. I don't know how you do it, Kendra. Blake is so supportive. You're so lucky. I'll help you all I can." Daphne got up from the table to get herself a drink. "Aunt Edna and Aunt Ruby are supposed to come down soon. Aunt Edna had a tooth get infected or something, so they're waiting until she feels better. Want some?" She offered some orange juice as she poured it into her glass. Kendra shook her head no. "I swear they call me all the time. They are planning to stay here, and I keep telling them I can't drive them back and forth all the time and that it was over an hour to Mom's. They don't hear me though." She returned to the table and sat beside Kendra. "I talked with Mathew and Ronnie, gave them all the updates."

"Daphne, what are you telling them?"

"I tell them she's doing okay. She's still her same old self. You know how she's always saying she can't eat?"

"Yeah."

"Well, she came out here for dinner and she ate like a pig. A pig, Kendra. She was shoving everything in her mouth, and when my friend Andrea said something to her, she suddenly had to throw it all up, claimed she was just trying, and had to get her oxygen. I just can't tell how much is for attention and how much is real."

Kendra laughed. *Yep, that's our mother*, she thought. It was funny, and yet she could see Daphne's exasperation. She put up with a lot more than Kendra would ever have patience for.

The rest of the evening was spent in a companionable sisterhood. They reminisced about childhood experiences, with Daphne doing most of the talking. *It's funny,* Kendra thought, *that most of our shared memories are before I turned ten years old.* Not too many memories after that. Of course, by the time she was ten, Daphne had been fourteen and already working a job as a waitress.

Kendra also found humor in how the entire family would tell stories and then look at her and say, "You remember that, don't you?" Considering she was the baby, she didn't remember much of it, if any. Some of it actually happened before she was born, and yet she was somehow expected to remember. Maybe she had magical powers she had yet to unleash, she would tease.

She was able to return home once again with a confidence that her mom was okay for now, her sister was definitely in denial and overwhelmed, and that she still had time before needing to come out to stay. She was glad she had taken the time for the trip, and she was glad to arrive back home. Home, where she could enjoy her husband and animals and get back to a routine she knew and welcomed.

CHAPTER 9

The summer progressed with no outstanding events. Kendra was thankful for the quiet time. It lasted just long enough to help her forget that she was waiting for the other shoe to drop. Then the call came. Elaine, from hospice called and asked that Kendra make arrangements to come soon. Not that it needed to be right now, just in the next few weeks.

Kendra prepared for her prolonged stay in Phoenix. As she was making mental plans and preparing her team from work, an opportunity arose to assist a friend get to El Paso. Jenny had returned to Texas from her assignment in Japan and wanted to make the trip to Phoenix to see her grandma, too. Since she was planning to drive to Phoenix, a drive that was certainly nineteen hours or more, she decided to wait until Jenny was able to take leave and accompany her.

She loaded up her cosmetics, her friend, her daughter, and herself and finally started making the trip in early August. They sang on the ten-hour drive to El Paso. They talked, laughed, and rode in companionable silence. After dropping her friend in El Paso, Kendra and Jenny continued on their way.

Jenny talked most of the way, bringing her mom up to date on her happenings while in Japan, her stay in San Diego, her boyfriends, girlfriends, and life in general. Kendra was thankful for the never-ending litany of life experience. It prevented her from sinking too far into the negative or the self-pity of having to do this task. About the time they reached Los Cruces, Kendra was beginning to feel restless. It was early evening, and if she did the math correctly, that would put them in Phoenix at about 2:00 a.m.

"Do you want to stop somewhere and continue in the morning?" Kendra asked Jenny, who had started to drift into a restless sleep.

"If you want to, I'm okay with that," she replied sleepily.

"I'll call Mom and let her know. I don't see why we should knock ourselves out trying to get there tonight when we can arrive fresh and alert tomorrow."

"Mom? Hey. How's it going?" Kendra said into the phone.

"Okay, honey. Where are you? Is everything okay?"

"I'm okay. We're in Los Cruces. You sure you're okay? You sound funny."

"Yes, honey. I'm just tired is all. I took my meds about thirty minutes ago, and they always make me sound drowsy. What time do you think you'll be here?"

"I was thinking we might stop and finish the drive tomorrow. Is that okay, or do you want us there tonight?" Kendra was trying to sound upbeat in a matter-of-fact way.

"Oh." There was a long pause. "Okay, well, you do what you have to then."

Kendra could hear the disappointment in her mother's voice. It wasn't quite fear, yet it had a fear edging. It wasn't really loneliness, yet she could tell her mom did not want to be alone. She suddenly had the feeling it was imperative to continue driving so they could arrive tonight. Not fully understanding the feeling within her, she could glean that much from it. They would continue.

"Well, you get some rest, and we'll see you soon. I love you." Her mom made a small noise, and the line disconnected.

"We're going to go on through tonight, Jenny. I can't explain why, I just know we need to be there. Do you think we should call Janie and let her know?"

"If you want to call her, call her, Mom. I'm not calling her." Kendra was surprised at the sharp retort and wondered what had transpired between these two again. There seemed to always be something that kept those around Janie on edge.

"I'll call her then," Kendra said. "Hello, Janie? It's your mom.

"Hey, Mom, wassup?"

"I just thought I'd let you know that I'm on my way to Phoenix to stay this time. Mom doesn't sound too good, and hospice asked me to come." There was no emotion in Kendra's voice. It was flat, monotone, and unfeeling.

Janie's reply was similar. "Okay, tell her I love her. By the way, she said I could have her curio cabinet and her dishes, the good set. Do you think you could bring them back for me? I'll figure out a way to get them from you."

Shocked at the request, Kendra was true to her word. "No. I'm not a storage facility for anything that Mom is giving away. You want it, you figure out a way to get it. I'll let you know when it becomes available. Bye." And with that, she hung up.

They arrived at Kathleen's door shortly before 3:00 a.m. Kendra rang the doorbell before realizing that she had the keys to her mom's apartment somewhere. Actually, she was a little surprised that the door wasn't ajar to allow for the cats. Her door was always open. Feeling a fear creep into her abdomen, she started digging for the keys as the door opened.

Kathleen had shrunk. And she had aged even more. Jenny acted as if she saw no difference, allowing Kendra time to adjust. The relief was obvious on her face as Kathleen wrapped her arms around her granddaughter. Kendra said a silent prayer, thanking the Lord for letting them arrive safely, and more importantly, for letting her know she needed to get here.

The hide-a-bed was almost completely pulled out, with only the last fold to set on the floor that would block the front door. It was made with nice blankets, fluffy pillows, and even a glass of water on each side of the bed. Her mom had been prepared even though she was in pain.

Making up her mind that she needed to continue as if things were normal, Kendra immediately changed her tone to the dutiful daughter and tucked her mother back in bed.

Jenny left for Albuquerque the next day while Kendra went to work in Phoenix since the company she worked with had offices there. She tried working from her mom's apartment, only to find herself frustrated by midday. The network connection was unreliable, and every time she dialed into a conference call, it seemed her mom would turn up the television. Kendra could not concentrate on her calls while listening to Geraldo or Andy Griffith in the other ear.

Kathleen would visit with her many friends the entire time that Kendra hid in the kitchen on conference calls. One day she overheard their conversation.

"What does Kendra do for this company?" Phyllis asked Kathleen.

"I can't tell. She talks a lot, tells them what to do, and recites a bunch of numbers," came Kathleen's confused, frustrated reply. It was obvious she wanted her daughter's attention while her daughter obviously tried to ignore the situation.

Kendra was spiraling out of control. She couldn't concentrate on work, she couldn't even think about cosmetics, and she couldn't watch her mom disappear. The memories from her dad dying came back vividly. That was the introduction to cancer for Kendra. That is when she realized that it just took you away from those who love you a little at a time, dying in slow motion while your family stood by watching, helpless to stop it, unable to ignore it. *I'm not a caregiver; what am I doing here with my mother now?* she thought angrily to herself. She was feeling extremely helpless and did not want to disappoint her mother as the last act before she was gone.

Then came calls from the family. Her aunts would call and ask questions. Her sister would call and ask questions. Her cousins would call and ask questions. Not her brothers though. They didn't call.

Finally, in an effort to reduce the amount of explanations, phone calls, and frustration, Kendra decided to start a blog. This would keep her family informed without the interaction. Hopefully.

It had been Blake's idea actually. She missed him. Often she would forget about the time differences and miss an opportunity to call him. They always sent text messages though. Right now, she needed to hear his voice.

"Hey, Blake. How you doing with me gone?" Kendra asked with a smile on her face. Not that it fooled her husband for a moment.

"How are you doing is the real question. You doing okay? Do you need anything?"

"I'm okay. Daphne and I cleared a spot in Mom's room yesterday so I could put an air mattress down that she bought for me instead of sleeping on the couch. Mom was talking with Phyllis in the living room while we did it. After a while, she just couldn't remain calm and started getting upset. Daphne managed to calm her and convince her we weren't getting rid of anything, just storing some of the holiday things so I could sleep in there."

"That's your mom. Who's Phyllis? The neighbor?"

"Yeah, she's the lady next door that does everything with mom. I think they're best friends or something."

"Oh, ok. I can't keep up with all her friends, sorry."

"Neither can I. She comes and goes. Some days she's really good, and I wonder why I'm here. Other days, she pretty much sleeps all day, waking up to take her meds and then back to sleep. She's so strong. I hope I'm that strong when my time comes."

"Don't talk like that. You can't leave me, so just don't even think that way," Blake replied quickly.

"I started a blog like you suggested to keep the family informed. It helps me." Kendra tried to sound positive and encouraging to him. She could hear the concern in his voice and wanted somehow to assuage his fears. "It's funny," Kendra continued, "looking back. You may think of your parents as a pain to your lifestyle. That they do not understand your creativity, your dreams, your desires, your beliefs, and the list goes on and on. I had an epiphany—I don't understand theirs either. I wonder how many other children don't really see their parents. I thought I knew my mom pretty well. Lately, I can see that part of her that just wants to be the little girl, the part that wants to be Cinderella, the part that just wanted to be beautiful and loved. Do you think she felt loved from Dad in this way?"

"Of course she did; why else would she be willing to let go?"

"I'm so glad that I have that kind of love from you. You are my prince charming, you know that, right?"

"Yes, dear," Blake replied with laughter, "and I'm also your Charlie!" Charlie was the name he had been given when they first started dating. Kendra had insisted that all men were dogs, and if he had to be a dog, then he would be Charlie from *All Dogs Go to Heaven*, and she would be his Cindy, not his Cindy Brady, but his Cinderella.

As she hung up the phone, she sat on the porch swing enjoying the night air. Her dad's seventy-sixth birthday was just around the corner on October 16; her sister Jo's fifty-fifth birthday was on October 15. She wondered if her mom would make it past their birthdays. She had said that she was ready to go and had described her current state as not living, nor dying—she was existing—and that it was a horrible place to be.

Kendra had witnessed her losing track of days and events. *Then again*, she thought, *don't we all?* Her mom at least had good reason being recently put on liquid morphine as needed, to accompany the pill form she was already taking.

In the six days since she had arrived with Jenny, she had seen good days and bad days. On good days, Kathleen was awake and lucid for several hours at a time. She would take naps throughout the day, mostly short ones. They would have interesting conversations during her good days. On her bad days, she would sleep all day. The few minutes she would be awake were often minutes of frustration and confusion. Kendra kept looking for the anger, but it wasn't anger she witnessed. It was frustration because she couldn't remember. She couldn't remember days, people, events, nothing, and she would become frustrated and anxious. Kendra tried to understand the frustration; not being able to remember things would frustrate anyone.

Sometimes on her good days Kendra would watch her and wonder, *Why am I here now; she has a long time left?* Upon closer examination, though, she could see her pallor was gray, ashy even. And if she watched closely, she would see her stumble to the side and hold on to furniture as she moved through her tiny apartment.

She allowed her thoughts to drift to family. When was the last time they saw her, really saw her, as Kathleen the woman, Kathleen the person? Are they ready for her to be gone with no last comments? Are they so busy in their respective worlds that they don't have time for her?

Is what they're doing today *that* important they can't spare a phone call or take a couple days out of a lifetime to say good-bye? Kendra wasn't angry. She recognized it was their choice. She had always recognized and tried her best to respect other people's freedom of choice. She knew at the end of the day, they would be the one living with that decision. Her choice was to be with her mom, holding her hand, crying with her, reassuring her, and giving her permission to leave if that is what she needed.

"God, please be merciful to her," Kendra prayed. "Thank you for allowing me to be here, for my job that gives me this flexibility, and for my husband who supports me being here. Thank you for a husband that loves me and for the temple where I have been sealed to my mother for eternity. Lord, please let the family see and read the blog. Please have those contact me that have questions or touch their hearts so there is no fighting after. Lord, please don't let her suffer long. In Jesus's name I pray. Amen."

CHAPTER 10

Kendra awoke early to prepare for work. She was quiet so she did not disturb her mother. She had decided to work the early shift in the local office for several reasons. First, it allowed her to avoid the rush-hour traffic in Phoenix. Second, it kept her on the same schedule with her team back home. Third, it reduced the anxiety that Kathleen felt. Kendra was not oblivious to her mother's guilt. Kathleen could not understand her job and as a result would attempt to avoid being in the same room. Only she had nowhere to go except her chair, and that made Kendra uncomfortable.

On her drive to work, Kendra reflected on her mother's behavior, conversations she had witnessed, and how she dealt with people in general. It was amazing to watch her. She put so much thought into making people feel comfortable. Her whole life she and her siblings—in fact, anyone who knew Kathleen—would make jokes about how she always changed the facts to a story. It was truly funny what she would choose to change. Looking at it from inside, Kendra now believed that she did it on purpose. She changed the stories to make those listening feel more comfortable. Whether it meant leaving out important facts or literally making them up out of the blue, she would. Funnier yet was that she saw nothing wrong in doing so; she was fully cognizant of her fabrications.

It was the frustration that worried Kendra and that Kathleen insisted on calling herself stupid all the time. Kendra wanted to just reach over and smack her mom when she did that, feeling more like the parent than the child. She had to keep reminding herself that it wasn't stupidity her mother felt; it was frustration.

It was a good day at work, and Kendra felt that it would be a good time to visit Daphne. Perhaps stop at Dairy Queen and get her mom a root beer float, her favorite. She had noticed that her mom wasn't eating much, so calories of any kind would probably be good.

Kathleen sounded surprised and elated when she received the phone call from Kendra that held the invitation to visit Daphne. Kendra knew how much Kathleen truly enjoyed the visits to Daphne's, and it sounded like she was having a good day. Kathleen sounded strong, more like herself. Today was one of those days that Kendra felt hospice was wrong; her mom had plenty of time left.

As Kendra drove home to pick up her mom, she called Daphne to confirm the trip. "Hey, sista. How you doin'?" she asked in the voice made so popular by Joey in the show *Friends*.

"I just finished a load of laundry and was getting ready to call you. I had to clean the barn area this morning and catch up on my mail; it's just been piling up since I make it a point to see Mom so much. What's going on down there? Everything okay?"

Kendra just laughed; her sister would never change, always busy, busy.

"It's a good day today. Sometimes I wonder if there's anything wrong with Mom and today is one of those times. Wait…is that your voice I hear coming out of my mouth?" Kendra replied, poking fun at the situation. She wished she could be as optimistic as Daphne could or just blind or in denial, whatever the case was. Her heart wanted the comment to be right even though her head knew it to be wrong.

"Ha, ha, you're so funny. You know there's always more than one truth to any situation. When did you become so negative anyway? You didn't used to be."

"I'm just teasing, Daph; don't get defensive. We'll be up in a couple hours if that's okay with you. I'm just leaving work heading home, depending on what I see when I get there will depend on how quickly we head your way."

"Is she eating, Kendra?" Daphne asked.

"Now that you ask, I worry about how much she eats, or should I say doesn't eat. And before you comment, no, it's not my cooking. I'm not a calorie counter, but if I had to guess, I'd say she's eating less than two hundred calories a day."

"I told you she always eats up here, haven't I?"

"Yes, Daphne, you have. Mom always tells Kendera that she's drinking those Ensure drinks, but she's not. She might drink about four sips or so at a time, and that's only two to three times a day. The calories actually come from the popsicles she eats." Hearing nothing but silence instead of interruption, Kendra decided to get in as much information as she could. "I went shopping yesterday and bought some of her favorite foods, which didn't add up to much, but it was something." Discouragement mixed with laughter resounded in her dialogue to Daphne. Kendra was feeling the reality and trying her best to stay positive. If there was anything her mom did not need, it was negativity. *After all*, she thought, *if Mom can be strong through cancer, then I can certainly be positive when it comes to her.*

The drive to the mountains was nice. Kendra could tell her mom was feeling good by the mood she was demonstrating. The weather wasn't too horribly hot, and it was tempting to drive with the windows down. *How many more trips could she make before it was impossible?* Kendra wondered.

"Not to upset your good mood, Mom, but I was wondering, why did you choose me as your executor?"

"Because you're good with details, and regardless of how you feel, you can stay focused on the facts and not the emotions."

"How do you know that? You've never really seen me do anything."

"Kendra, do you think a mother is blind? Don't you see things your children do?"

"I guess so. I don't know, though, if it's the same as what you're talking about."

"Kendra, I hear you on that phone meeting after meeting, rambling off numbers, details, instructions, and giving praise all at the same time. You not only give them the step-by-step, you give them the big picture that is affected. That tells me that you understand how they feel and give them what they need without it affecting how you feel."

"And you see that as a good thing?"

"I read once that human nature doesn't accept the obvious until it can no longer be truly avoided. That describes Daphne. She will ignore anything that does not suit her purpose. You, you deal with everything, in your own time, in your own way."

"You think so, huh?" Kendra was incredulous. She would never have imagined that her mom paid that much attention to her or that she would come to those conclusions.

"Where are my pills? You know I won't make it very long if we forgot those." Kathleen asked almost in a panic.

"I have them, Mom."

"All of them? Not just my Darvocet, right? I need all my pills."

"I have all of them; relax." *Now if I just understood which ones you take when*, Kendra thought.

While Daphne and her mom visited and played with the dogs, Kendra stepped outside to call Sandy and bring her up to date.

"Isn't it funny how the Lord puts us in the exact place we need to be in when we need to be there, Sandy? It occurred to me on the drive up to my sister's that maybe this isn't even about Mom."

"What do you mean?" Sandy asked.

"Maybe it's about throwing those bricks at me and having a good time doing it. I can picture Him now, conversing with the other angels on who can hit me first or with the largest brick." Kendra was being blasphemous; she liked to assimilate the Lord as a normal, everyday person. Sandy knew this and enjoyed the rhetoric.

"Maybe He's just trying to show you that you *are* a caregiver, in your own way with your own talents. Maybe He's trying to show you that you contribute something in this complex world by listening, reading, telling stories, or telling your silly jokes. Of course, you have no problem giving tough love, but I know you are more a caregiver than you want to admit, Kendra."

"Whatever you say, Sandy. The good news is that I have not seen that vacant look all day, and that made my day. We're going to finish watching this movie tonight if she's up to it when we leave Daphne's. It's only taken us three days so far!" Kendra felt lighter; Sandy always had a way of doing that for her. "Anyway, just wanted to keep you posted. I'll call you tomorrow, okay? It's getting dark, and I don't like to drive at night."

"Okay, holler if you need me, Kendra; I mean it," Sandy said. Kendra just laughed and hung up the phone.

The rest of the visit went well. The hidden undertones that Kendra so often heard when they were all together didn't seem to be there this time. Daphne was attentive, watchful. Several times Kendra thought that Daphne saw the deterioration in their mother. Several times, she saw the look of sorrow in Daphne's eyes. It was unspoken, but Kendra was sure they all felt that this was Kathleen's last visit to Big Ranch Wannabe.

Kendra relayed the day's events to Blake before going to bed. His support and love came through with everything he said and didn't say. Sometimes just hearing his voice was all she needed. Kendra shared her observations about Daphne and her fear that maybe she too was in denial. He reassured her that it was a normal feeling to wish her Mom wasn't dying, to fantasize that she was not was all part of the process. His reassurance helped to restore peace once again to Kendra's soul enabling her to have a dreamless sleep that night.

Exasperated, Kendra just needed to get out. Deciding to work from the office instead of the apartment did not give her the relief she so desperately wanted. After being at the office for almost ten hours, she burned herself on the screens that supposedly protected the interior of the car from the heat; she had forgotten the effects of the heat in Phoenix. Anxious to get home, and check on her mom had made her careless in removing the screens from the windshield. Finally reaching the apartment, she discovered today of all days, her mom decided to clean out the refrigerator and throw away all the good food, leaving the bad food in tact! If all of that weren't bad enough, she had also decided to do Kendra's laundry, only she had forgotten and instead asked her friend Katie to put the items in the dryer on high, ruining many of her clothes. When she confronted her mom about these things, Kathleen had taken on the stricken look of a child that had just been yelled at. Kendra just needed out for a short time.

Finding an excuse to find the local post office, Kendra called Katie to come watch her mom and left. She didn't blame her mom; a few clothes could easily be replaced, and food could always be purchased. She was just feeling the stress. Trying to keep her day job going, watch over her mom, looking for *the* signs, and keeping the family up to date was weighing on her. The blog was helping, just not enough. She didn't want help because it would take her time away from her mom. She didn't want to admit that she needed help because that would make her seem incapable. She needed an outlet, though, and doing errands was as good as any.

When she returned back at the apartment, everything felt immediately calmer. Her mom was relaxing in her chair just inside the door, watching *Little House on the Prairie*.

"I thought Katie was going to stay with you until I got back?" Kendra asked as she entered the apartment.

"She was, but I sent her home. I like her and all; it's just sometimes I don't want her here. I was feeling fine anyway. Are you done being upset with me?"

"I'm not upset with you, Mom. I'm sorry I was uptight earlier, just a long day at work." Kendra sat down and started watching the show. She had forgotten the shows she grew up with. These shows taught right from wrong and encouraged hope and faith. The shows on television in modern day were all about dysfunctional families and children who disrespected their parents. Curling up on the couch, she took her mother's hand and just held it while they watched the rest of the show.

By the time the show ended, Kathleen was feeling restless. "Let's go for a walk." She stated getting up and reaching for the door. *Wow, that was fast.* Kendra thought. *That's the fastest and smoothest I've seen her move in days.* Kendra saw her flinch from the pain in an inconspicuous manner. Realizing that her mom wanted to pretend there was no pain, she didn't mention it. Instead, she just followed her outside, linking arms as she walked.

Kendra walked silently beside her mom. They had walked the perimeter of the apartment complex from gated entrance to gated entrance. Her mom led the way and decided the direction that literally had taken them from fence line to fence line. She wondered if subconsciously her mom was feeling trapped or boxed in. She was no psychology major, but she believed this behavior was indicative of something.

"I think I was a bit anxious today from being by myself all day." Kathleen suddenly broke the silent thoughts of her daughter. "I used to enjoy living alone. Now, I don't think I like it so much."

"You don't have to say sweet nothings to keep me here, Mom, I'm here for you," Kendra said jokingly.

Kathleen reached out and took her daughter's hand, lightly squeezing it.

This is nice, Kendra thought. *This is how I used to feel when we were together, Mom, when I was little. I love you so much.*

Phyllis came by the next morning before Kathleen was awake. She took the opportunity to talk with Kendra out of earshot. "Kathleen is doing so much better with you here, Kendra. You need to know that. She was going downhill fast." Phyllis was pacing in the kitchen, one step each direction. "I was afraid you wouldn't get here in time. She said you were coming on the tenth, and then the seventeenth, and then you didn't show until the nineteenth; she was getting worried."

"Phyllis, I never gave Mom a date when I was coming. I guess she was making them up on her own. I said I would call her when I left and that it would be after the middle of the month," Kendra responded defensively from the small kitchen table.

"Have you talked with hospice lately? I asked them to call you. They are always saying that family members can work miracles just by being present, so I told them to call. Not to wait."

"I spoke with them the other day but not about that. I just wanted to make sure what medications she was supposed to be taking and how often. As you know, she doesn't always keep track of her thoughts, days, times, or conversations, but she knows when it's time for her meds, and she is taking the right doses at the right time. I wonder if that is how ingrained the nurse is in her."

While Kendra was joking, Phyllis was extremely solemn. Making another attempt to lighten the mood, Kendra changed the topic.

"My cousin called yesterday, and Mom talked for less than five minutes. She didn't seem too interested, or maybe the phone is difficult for her now. I don't think she's up to many visitors either. Of course, you are always welcome, Phyllis, especially when I need a break, okay?" Kendra thought maybe a hug would help, only she couldn't get herself to reach out.

"Well, I can see your mom isn't aware all the time, and you can bet I won't be coming around to stare at her; she's afraid that's what people will do, and I promised I wouldn't.

"Interesting," Kendra responded, even though Phyllis didn't seem to hear her.

"If you need something, you call though. I need to get going; tell her I stopped by." And she was out the door. Kendra was a little puzzled at the quickness of her departure and just shook her head and went to check on her mom.

She had no sooner stepped into the living room when the phone rang. Reaching to grab it before it rang a second time, she quickly whispered, "Hello?"

"Hey, sista. How you doin'?"

"Daphne, why are you calling the house phone? Why not call my cell so it's not so loud?"

"Oh, I thought I was calling your cell, I'm sorry. I wasn't paying attention. How's Mom?"

"She's sleeping. We had a good night last night. We walked all over the complex, and when we got home she ate! She ate a lot! She had one and a half White Castle hamburgers; as gross as those are, she gobbled them right up. By the looks of the kitchen, she also ate some orange ice cream, and she must have eaten her lunch because there's no sign of it anywhere, unless she gave it away or threw it out with the rest of the good food from the fridge." Laughing, Kendra continued to give a good report and then reminded her sister to check the blog for a true update.

It was grand central station for Kendra. As soon as she hung up the phone from talking with her sister, her cell phone rang. It was her son, Jerry.

"Hey, boy. Wassup?" Kendra teased.

"Nothing. How are you doing?"

"Me? I'm *fabuloso*, of course. How else would I be?" she teased.

"I was reading your blog, and I see that Grandma had a good day. You know, I see this a lot working in senior care. The patients light up completely when family comes and visits. I think Grandma is doing better because you're there."

"Oh, you do. What do you want?" Kendra asked with that suspiciously humorous tone parents often use when they are complimented by their children.

"Seriously. They may be out of their minds, but they know and keep track of who comes to visit whom. I just wanted to tell you that I think you're doing great. And if you didn't know it, you're also in the role of messenger. Can you tell her that Mel and I love her and we're thinking about her?" Jerry said in a more solemn tone.

"Of course I'll tell her. I don't want her thinking that you forgot about her after all she's done for you. She knows you love her."

Silence.

"I'm just teasing, you know."

"I have to clock in now; just wanted to call real quick and tell you great job, Mom! Love you; talk to you later." And with that Jerry hung up.

Kendra waited to see if another phone would ring before continuing on her trek to the bedroom.

CHAPTER 11

Kendra groaned as she thought she heard a knock on the door. She listened for a moment. Nothing. As she rolled over to return to blissful sleep, her cell phone rang. Quickly she grabbed it. "Hello?"

"Hey, Mom. Can you open the door please?"

"What?"

"I'm out front; can you open the door please?"

"What time is it?"

"Eight thirty. Please?" Jenny said. "I really, really need to go, if you know what I mean."

"Yes, be right there." Kendra hung up and went to roll out of bed when it registered that Jenny had said eight thirty. *Oh, no*, she thought, *I had a meeting thirty minutes ago.* Struggling to focus on her phone to dial while quietly exiting the bedroom, she opened the front door.

"Thank you!" Jenny exclaimed in a whisper as she quickly headed through the bedroom to the bathroom.

Just as her meeting was ending, her mom was waking up. Jenny was in there talking with her, so Kendra just made another cup of herbal tea and sat down to read her e-mails. She had another meeting starting soon. As she opened her e-mail, she thought, *Great, now those two are talking, and I have another call. I don't like work-*

ing from here. If I leave though, Mom gets anxious; if I stay, she gets frustrated. How's that go, half of one and six of the other...wait, now I sound like Mom. Six of one and half a dozen of the other.

The hospice nurse, Kendera, stopped by shortly after Kendra admitted defeat on staying focused for any business call. They discussed her anxiety, and Kathleen was prescribed two more prescriptions to help manage the anxiety. Jenny and Kendera were having an in-depth discussion on the topic and came up with an answer. Kendra sat at her computer listening and laughing at their "women logic." As she continued reading her personal e-mail, their logic was confirmed in her "Daily Kick in the Butt" message from *Runner's World*:

> Frustration is the first step toward improvement. I have no incentive to improve if I'm content with what I can do and if I'm completely satisfied with my pace, distance, and form as a runner. It's only when I face frustration and use it to fuel my dedication that I feel myself moving forward.
>
> John "The Penguin" Bingham

"That makes perfect sense," Kendra said as she read the note aloud. "Mom is feeling frustrated because she can't remember things. She's really making a concerted effort to pay attention and remember which is making her anxious, which is rubbing off on me, which rubs off on her, and round and round we go. If I go running, I'll be too tired to get on this hamster wheel!"

Throughout the day, Kathleen would drift off occasionally. She had visitors and phone calls intermittently. Of course, she had Jenny there all day, and by 7:00 p.m.

she was exhausted. Kendra knew she was fading when she didn't even want to talk to her baby boy, Ronnie, whom she knew her mom had been waiting to hear from. She explained as best she could to her older brother and wrote in her blog for the family to understand.

> Please don't take it personally if she doesn't talk when you call; she is just exhausted and hurting. She does love each one of you. She really wants to see you and gets frustrated because she knows she couldn't stand it if you all appeared. When there are more than two people in the room, she can't keep up, and so she begins to shut down. I guess it takes too much energy. She is afraid, and yet she faces each day with a new determination to do something meaningful and remember it. She is in pain, and yet she gets up every day. She walks around every day. She does some menial task or chore every day, no matter how much it hurts. Today, she practically crawled underneath her porch swing to pick up a half-eaten bird and throw it in the trash. I *know* that hurt, but her determination is more powerful than her pain. She is such a fascinating woman. I'm proud to be her daughter!

"Hello?" Kendra answered the phone yet again. She was beginning to feel like this phone line was connected to some worldwide device that others could see, showing them each time the line was free so someone else could make it ring.

"Hey, cuz. It's Lisa. I've been reading your blog, and I just wanted you to know I'm with you. You are so in tune."

"Thanks, Lisa; you don't know how much I need to hear that right now."

"I remember all this when my mom passed away. I've been speaking to a few of the family members now. It still puzzles me when they ask, 'Do you think I should go see her now, or do you think I can wait a while yet?'"

Kendra chuckled in a nonhumorous way. This was the frustration she tried to avoid her entire life. *The family*, as Lisa put it, was nothing but drama and self-centeredness. Instead of fighting it, she simply chose to avoid it.

"I guess to be quite frank and to the point, my question back is, 'Wait for what? What don't you understand about a diagnosis of terminal cancer? This disease gets progressively more and more painful. What are you waiting for? She was diagnosed over a year ago and you haven't been to see her yet? What are you waiting for? She has fewer and fewer good days. What are you waiting for? She grows less tolerant of entertaining company. What are you waiting for? The longer you wait to see her, the harder it's going to be on you to witness her pain and discomfort."

"So, what are they waiting for?"

"I told them that I understand that times are hard on a lot of us right now, and they may not be able to afford the trip. That's totally understandable to everyone. We're not all going to get to go out and visit with her before she passes; just please take the time to send a card with a note. Make a call, and don't be disappointed if she does not feel up to visiting on the phone sometimes."

"She would love a card more than a phone call right now."

"I was fortunate enough to have been able to go out last fall and have a nice visit with her. We both knew that was the last time we were going to see each other. I still remember the hug good-bye at the airport. I will miss her stories. I told them if you call and she's up to story telling, count yourself lucky. My Auntie K was very comforting to me during a difficult time in my life when my mom was very ill. For that I will be forever thankful. It's time to make your peace and tell her you love her. What are you waiting for?"

"Wow, Lisa. I'm glad you're on my side!" Kendra laughed. "I couldn't have said all that better if I tried. Thank you!"

"No problem, cuz. You hang in there and let me know whenever you need to talk; I'm here."

"Well, in case anyone is interested, please let them know that Jenny and I checked out the local hotels, the ones that are a few miles from Mom's house. The Holiday Inn is the best and gives a discount under the circumstances. If you plan to come down, let me know, and I'll send you the manager's name so you can call and check it out."

"I'm not coming out again; I've already said my good-byes. I'll pass that along to the family though. Take care." And just like that, Lisa was gone.

Since Jenny was there, Kendra felt it safe to go to the office for a few hours the next morning without causing her mother anxiety. Perhaps between the new medication and her granddaughter being there, her own presence would not be missed.

It was a sight when she walked in the door later that day. Her mom was asleep in her chair, and Jenny was asleep on the couch, holding Kathleen's hand and leaning up against her chair. One of Kathleen's friends, Becky, was on the opposite end of the couch, and Phyllis was in the rocking chair beside the bedroom door. Phyllis and Becky were just talking away as if the other two beings in the room were not present at all. As politely as she could, Kendra asked the ladies to leave since her mom was not cognizant of their visit. Feeling a little protective of her mother, Kendra began to wonder how long before she had to be the bad guy and put a stop to all visitors.

Shortly after their exit, Kathleen awoke. She was struggling to hang on to the present. All she could focus on was her need for ice water, maybe a little food too. After two bites of melon, she was exhausted and just wanted to go to bed. Making her way in as much a dignified manner as she could muster, she retreated to her bedroom and shut out the world once again on her way to oblivion.

Stepping back into the living room, Kendra saw Jenny was awake as well.

"Hey, Jenny. How was the day?" Kendra asked as she assumed her mother's position in the chair.

"It was good. She did real good, and then I guess we both got really tired. Did I hear people here?"

"You mean you didn't know they were here? How long have you two been sleeping?"

"I don't know; we were watching *All in the Family*."

"Wow, I'd say judging by the time it had to have been a couple hours."

"How you doing, Mom? You look tired."

"I've been doing a lot of thinking today. It dawned on me that every time I hear a story from the family about Mom, it's about a forty-five-year-old story. I don't think too many of them know the woman I know." Kendra made her self comfortable in her mother's chair, tucking her feet up under her. "Think about it. She raised at least six kids and multiple foster kids. She cooked, she cleaned, she worked, she ironed, she sewed, and she took care of the elderly."

"Yeah, she's quite the woman, reminds me of someone," Jenny interjected grinning, yet lovingly looking at her mother as if it was obvious to whom she referred.

Ignoring her, Kendra continued, "I remember a couple elderly women whom Mom cared for each day. She would cook them meals, clean their houses, bathe them, keep them company, hold their hands, and do whatever was necessary for a few hours a day. I remember playing outside most of the time she would visit these women because her endless talking was the most boring thing on earth to me then. Sort of like mine is to you." She winked at her youngest daughter. Jenny just held her hand and watched her, silently urging her to continue.

"Mom instilled in her children a strong work ethic. I raised you three children by myself, and I cannot even comprehend how Mom worked with so many all the time. She and Dad normally worked different shifts, probably to avoid daycare costs, so it amounted to something like a single parent. At least it was only one of them home at a time."

Jenny squeezed her mother's hand, her eyes watering slightly.

"I believe all of us children have a strong sense of human kindness." Kendra continued. "I mean, if we see someone in need, we try to help. We offer charity to others in the true sense of the word. And we do it because it was the example set before us our whole lives. We may not have had much growing up, and what we had was shared with anyone who needed a roof over their head or food in the belly. Like you said about me that time I asked you what you thought my top values were, remember? You said that you'd like to tell me family, but the truth was that you knew I'd treat a stranger off the street the same as I would treat you. Well, now you know where I learned that from."

"And I know where I learned it from." Jenny smiled.

"All six of us kids that grew up together either are or have been entrepreneurs, successful entrepreneurs too. That says that she raised us with a sense of individuality and courage.

"Like you did us."

"None of us have been afraid to step out and try what we believed in. She instilled *dreams* in us, taught us how to dream, and showed us the determination to make them come true."

"Like you did."

"I remember living in rundown places. I remember living in too small of places and having powdered milk mixed with real milk to make it last longer. I remember that awful block cheese from welfare and greasy peanut butter."

"Like I do."

"And yet, just a few short years ago, she and Dad owned their own house here, their own home. It was a nice home, with nice furniture and nice decorations, a camper where they spent a lot of their time, and good friends. Through all her hardships, she knew how to make any house a home and she finally got her dream."

"Also, like you did. Don't you see that you're as special to me as she is to you? That's why you're my best friend." Jenny leaned over the arm of the chair and rested her head on Kendra's forearm.

"Above all, I would say that she is a loving mom. Through all the chores, laundry, cooking, jobs, and demands, she found time to attend school functions. She attended football games and concerts, plays and graduations. And in all that time, she continued to take in children and care for the elderly.

Jenny just listened.

"She instilled faith in each one us. While we have all gone off into our own religions, it was Mom's insistence that we attend church that put the gift of faith in our lives. She taught us prayer, hope, and humility. She taught us kindness and generosity.

"I don't know the woman many of her family speak about. She lived before I was born." Kendra was stroking Jenny's hair absentmindedly as she talked. "I only know the woman I watch today, the woman who made me who I am, who cried many nights wondering where I was and if I'd come home alive, the woman who punished me because she worried, the woman who picked me up at wee hours of the morning in places I don't remember because she said if I was ever in need, just call. She's the woman who took you kids in when I was struggling to find myself, the woman who has to stop at every animal and every child to say a kind word, give a treat, a pat, or a tickle. This is the woman I know. This is the woman I will miss. And most of all, this is the woman who taught me values that I pray my own children have learned and that they will pass on for generations to come.

Jenny leaned her face against her Mom's arm, squeezing her forearm for reassurance.

"She made me, and Blake polished me!" Kendra had tears gently streaming down her face as she brought herself back to the present moment. She was unaware she had been holding in all the emotion and love that she felt. She focused on her daughter and saw what could be her reflection. Jenny had tears streaking down her cheeks, and her eyes shone with such love. *If only I could hold this moment forever in suspended time*, Kendra thought, knowing all too soon it would be gone.

CHAPTER 12

The cooler temperature was quickly turning to a suffocating heat as the dawn of a new day overtook the valley. Kathleen was sleeping in her chair, as she did longer and longer with each new day. Walking back into the tiny apartment after seeing Jenny off in the shuttle to the airport, Kendra sat down in the glider rocker and just watched her mom. She was in her chair with her hands folded in her lap. Her head was hanging down in what must have been a most uncomfortable position. The cats would keep their distance and just watch their owner as well.

After a few minutes of observing, not really feeling, just taking it all in to process later, Kendra took a good look at her mother's hands. *Were they swollen?* she wondered. Looking at her feet and ankles convinced her that yes, she was swollen. Kendra located the paperwork about the new prescriptions her mother had started taking and after reading them contacted nurse Kendera.

While Kathleen was no longer anxious, she also was sleeping much more than what she had been before the medication change. One of the side effects of the new medication was drowsiness which was also a symptom of progression for her cancer. Technically, the natural progression was sleeping longer and more frequently. Looking at both the medication and her cancer having the same symptom only confused Kendra more. Nurse Kendera suggested taking her off the medication and confirmed with the doctor from hospice. Now it was a matter of waiting and watching.

Several hours had gone by before Kathleen awoke. She wasn't very lucid, but she was awake. Kendra tried having a conversation with her, only to realize it was a useless battle. It was at this moment that Kathleen's youngest sister, Judy, decided to check in. Kendra had never been close to her aunt Judy and, in fact, considered her to be the most self-centered of the entire family.

Seeing as Kathleen was unable to carry on a conversation, it was only a matter of minutes before she handed the phone back to her daughter.

"Hey, Aunt Judy," Kendra stated flatly.

"Hey, kiddo. So I'll be honest; I don't hear any difference in her. She sounds high but not sick. Is she really sick?"

"Yes, she's really sick. She's on liquid morphine as needed, and she's been on this other medication that we believe is adding to her drowsiness. I'm sorry she couldn't talk much today; it's not one of her better days." Kendra was not in a mood to entertain her aunt or to convince her of anything. *Let her believe what she wants*, she thought.

"Well, my mother-in-law has cancer, and it's eating away her internal organs. She doesn't sound like that."

"I don't know what to tell you, Aunt Judy. I don't know your mother-in-law. I can only tell you that morphine will probably make a person sound pretty high, as you put it." Having sufficiently had her button pushed, Kendra slowly began unleashing some of the anger that was building up inside of her.

"I'm truly sorry to hear about your mother-in-law's cancer throughout her body. I guess you haven't realized that your lymph system runs through your entire body? Tell me Aunt Judy, do you think cancer in the kidney feel any worse than cancer in your lymph system?"

"That's not—"

"Cancer is cancer. It is painful. I've known several people who have died from it, and morphine is normally the end drug due to those high levels of pain. Morphine as needed is about as liberal as it gets. I don't know if you meant the comparison or not; I certainly felt as if you were telling me that Mom couldn't possibly be as bad as your mother-in-law because she's only *high* and has lymphoma. I'm sorry you feel that way, and I am terribly sorry that your mother-in-law has to deal with cancer as well. I pray I never have it in any form."

"Kendra, I—"

"Thank you for calling her though. Mom has been keeping a log to record everyone who has called. And no, it's not a she-did, he-didn't type log. It's a log to help her remember that you did call her and the day she last spoke to you. And regardless of how irritable and nasty I sound right now, keep in mind that she records these things so when she is lucid she can recall everything that is precious and worth remembering for her."

"Kendra, that is *not* what I meant, and you know it. I have been through this before, and I know her a lot better than you do, kiddo. I'll let you go. I have to go pick up the kids anyway. Be sure to tell her I love her and I'm thinking of her. If that isn't too much to ask."

"I will, Aunt Judy. Thank you for calling."

Kendra hung up the phone and sat down on the sofa and dropped her head into her hands. Silently, she conversed with the Lord.

"Lord, I'll be the first to admit I'm really *trying* to be good-hearted about this with the family and keep everyone involved who cares to be. How can I get this to sink in at some level for them? That if it's not positive, it's negative? Do they know how self-righteous they come across? Is it them, Lord, or is it me? Am I being the self-righteous one? Am I subconsciously being the martyr, expecting them to respect me for all I'm doing? Please forgive me if I am.

"I'm so thankful I have this time with her. I'm thankful I have a husband who loves me, who supports me, understands me, and, more importantly, understands the things I feel I need to do. I'm thankful for my children and my grandchildren. I pray none of them ever have to watch me die slowly through this painful disease. And I pray I never have to watch them go through it. Stay with me, Lord; help me experience this with her in a dignified manner. In these things I pray in the name of Jesus Christ. Amen."

The next day Kendra awoke at almost noon; surprisingly, Kathleen was up and in her chair already. She was already mostly dozing in her chair with her friend Penny in the glider rocker. It kept Kendra amazed at the myriad of visitors and friends who continuously flowed through the tiny apartment. Her mother was certainly an appreciated and loved woman.

After Penny left, Kathleen awoke and said something about Phyllis coming by. Kendra just laughed and thought, *Whatever*, and continued with her day. Sure enough, not fifteen minutes later, Phyllis stopped by with breakfast: root beer floats for everyone! That was Kendra's kind of breakfast! The best part of the breakfast was her mom actually ate some of it. Not much, but a few bites, and that was enough to please Kendra.

The sugar in the ice cream must have given Kathleen a surge of energy or a craving for starch because she said she really craved a fried potato. Slowly, after standing from her chair, she made her way into the kitchen as both Kendra and Phyllis watched with surprised expressions. After finding a right-sized potato and finding her favorite peeling knife, she was only able to peel a fraction of the potato before she had to admit fatigue and called Kendra in to finish.

She retreated slowly back to her chair; she was able to stay awake long enough to eat a few pieces of the fried potato before drifting off again.

"Well, that was something!" Kendra said, smiling at Phyllis.

Phyllis didn't say anything and instead stood and patted her friend's hand, kissed her on the forehead, and excused herself from the apartment.

Understanding Phyllis's departure and not wanting to look at anything from her job, Kendra decided to start cleaning the apartment, starting with the tall bookcase just inside the door. It was filled with books and newspaper clippings. There was half a shelf of books and clippings about the cast from *The Sound of Music* and many items relating to the *Little House on the Prairie* series.

Her mom and sister Jo had loved that story. Kendra believed they could have both lived in that time and felt completely at home. Not her though; no, Kendra could not imagine living in a time with so few conveniences and having to wear a dress with all the underclothes day after day. Nope, she would have been an outlaw if she had lived in those days simply because she would have to wear the pants.

"What's so funny?" her mom asked in a raspy voice.

Startled, Kendra looked over to see she was being watched. "Nothing really. Just imagining how we each would survive on the prairie."

"What are you doing? You're not throwing anything out are you?"

"No, Mom, I'm just looking, cleaning, and making sure your name is in your books."

"Well, put some on the floor and let me help."

Kendra made light talk with her mother over the next hour or so while putting labels in her books and dusting. She was surprised to see her mom on the floor, but that was where she wanted to be. Mostly, Kathleen would hold a book, pet her cat, Callie, and reminisce about days gone by. While she brought up many events prior to the time Kendra was born, Kendra still assured her that it was remembered fondly.

It wasn't too long before Kathleen needed help getting off the floor and back to her chair. She quickly nodded off again. She awoke in the early evening, took her meds again, and made her way to bed.

Kendra was elated that she had shared that time with her mom. This was a woman she had not seen in years; perhaps she too was a woman her mom had not seen in years. Her thoughts were disturbed by the chiming of the cell phone; it was Daphne.

After sharing the events of the day with her sister, Kendra took a few moments to really thank and acknowledge her sister. She felt as if her eyes were being opened to a side of life she had never really seen before, and she had to share those things before they were lost.

"Daphne, I have to tell you I feel I am out here to help you as much as Mom. I think you have had to bear the worst of all this for the past year. Because you live here, everyone expects you to provide the information, make the decisions, be hospitable, and continue running your own life as well. I have to admit I feel bad because I also expected all that from you. I never really acknowledged that you also have a busy life. You manage your business and help with so many organizations. I'm very proud of what you have accomplished and your outlook on life. After having to share a room with me for so many years, it's amazing you are so optimistic all the time—or maybe that's why you are, huh?"

"Aw, thanks, sis, but I should be thanking you. You being here is helping me so much. And look at your life! I can't imagine living in your shoes. Tell you what, I'll come down tomorrow and give you some relief so you can go run or go to the office or whatever, just get out and have some time to yourself. I know you miss your family and your animals; I'd be lost without my animals. You are such an awesome little sister; I wouldn't trade you for almost anyone."

Together, they shared a few laughs before calling it a night with the promise of seeing each other the next day. For Kendra, it felt good to finally feel like an equal and not an insignificant warm body. She drifted off to sleep with a smile on her face.

It was Sunday. Kendra watched her mom sleeping in the chair, knowing there would be no church today. *Maybe we could get to Daphne's one more time*, she thought. No, on second thought, she didn't think her mom could sustain the visit with the rambunctious puppies. Besides, Daphne was coming down instead.

Kendra busied herself by cleaning the front porch. Since her mom had been feeding the pigeons for years, they still appeared twice a day waiting for food. Kendra didn't feed them, but it didn't stop them from hanging around the porch swing or the walkway. Just as she was finishing, Kathleen awoke again.

"Daphne's on her way down. How are you feeling today?" Kendra asked while gently touching her mother's forearm.

"Hmmm? Oh, I'm good. Daphne's coming, you said? Oh! Did you clean my porch? Thank you, thank you, thank you!" Kathleen had managed to use her daughter's arm to help her stand and was looking out the front door.

"Maybe I should get changed and cleaned up before she gets here."

"While you're doing that, I think I'll go check the mail. You sure you're okay? You won't need me?"

"No, honey, go ahead."

Kendra had just walked in the front door of the apartment when she heard Daphne walking up behind her.

"Hello, Momma! I hear you're an unstoppable, book-labeling machine!" Daphne made her usual grand entrance into the apartment.

"Oh, what kind of lies has Kendra been saying about me?"

"Evil ones, Mom. The most wicked kind of lies I could think of that would keep all the people willing to listen engaged," Kendra answered.

"Ugh, look at your feet, Momma. And your eyebrows! Wow, your eyebrows are getting really super long; they could double as eyelashes. Here, let me clean you up and take care of you. That heathen of a daughter you call baby girl doesn't do this girly stuff, but I'll do it for you." Daphne was busy gathering the pan to soak her mom's feet in Epsom salts, grabbing toenail clippers, and grooming scissors.

"Hey, I wear makeup now; that's a girl thing!" Kendra chimed in, defending her newly discovered femininity.

"So what have you been eating, Momma? I heard you have root beer floats here. Do you want some ice cream? "

"No, I don't want any right now. Phyllis brought those over earlier today, or was it yesterday? Oh, I don't know. I'm so stupid I can't even keep my days straight anymore."

"You're not stupid, Momma; you're overwhelmed is all. It happens to me too when Kendra's around." Laughing, she turned to her sister. "Kendra, get Mom her ice cream please; she needs to eat. Look at you, Momma, before too long you're going to weigh less than me!"

"She doesn't want the ice cream, Daphne."

"Just get it; she'll eat some."

At another time, Kendra would have been upset or rattled as her sister took charge. This time, she acquiesced. She could see the blatant denial on her sister's face and understood the need to pretend things were normal. By pampering her mom and forcing her to eat, Daphne could pretend that she wasn't sick at all. She made quite a bit of progress actually; she managed to get her mother to eat half a root beer float, a few green beans, some noodles, and then some marshmallows. It was funny—every time their mom would start to close her eyes, Daphne would say something to her and make her wake up again.

Seeing as Daphne sufficiently wore her mother out for the day, she easily convinced Kendra to stay the night in the mountains with her. Kendra needed the break, their mom would most likely sleep the entire night, and Daphne could use the company.

They made small talk during the drive, and after settling in themselves with a good movie, Kendra started to confide in her sister.

"I think Mom is on the downward slope. I was reading that pamphlet from hospice today. She's showing all the signs described for one to three months left and even some from the one to two weeks left. Don't get me wrong; I don't know; it could be another six weeks. It might be another two weeks."

"Really, you think so? Why? She seemed fine to me. Look how much she ate tonight. She'll eat more tomorrow and probably has at least another year or so."

Realizing her sister wasn't ready to hear this, she backed off. "You're right. I'm probably being too literal.

I just pray she doesn't end up in bed for weeks before slowly slipping away."

Changing the subject to ease her sister's mood, Kendra continued, "Jenny called me today. She was glad she got to spend some quality time with Mom. She said my cat misses me and put the phone to his ear. She was laughing because she said the cat heard my voice and immediately plopped down and rolled over wanting his belly rubbed. Animals are so silly."

"Tell me about it. Have you seen my kitty baby? Come here; I'll show you, and then I need to hit the sack, sista. I wake up at 5:00 a.m. regardless, and I don't know about you, but I'm exhausted!"

"Agreed, sista! Just no rolling yourself in the blankets!"

"I would never do that if you just curled up to me on your own! I'm not singing you to sleep though; I don't care how scared of ghosts you are."

"Ha! In your dreams, big sister."

Laughing like the sisters they used to be, they headed off to bed.

CHAPTER 13

After the normal ritual of feeding animals, taking showers, and getting dressed, Daphne and Kendra made their way back to the valley. The hospice nurse, Kendera, was coming by, and they wanted to be sure and be present in case she came early.

Kendra and Daphne enjoyed visiting with Kendera; it was unfortunate they did not meet under different circumstances. Kendra was just glad that their personalities all clicked, or as her mother had put it, Kendera could have easily been a member of the family. After listening to people tell her all her life that she *should* be more like her sister Daphne, Kendra was surprised to hear Nurse Kendera say that even though they were obviously sisters, their personalities were like night and day to each other.

"So what do you think, Kendera?" Daphne inquired. "How much time are we looking at? Kendra thinks she's on a downward spiral, listless, won't eat, etc., and yet when I'm here she eats; she talks; she's awake. I think she has several months left at least."

"I don't know, Daphne. I really can't say. Everyone is different," Kendera replied "I've seen patients that I thought for sure were on their last breath who lived another six months, and I've had patients who seemed too vibrant not make it through the night. Everyone is different."

"Yeah, but you gotta have some idea. You have experience in this field. I don't need a commitment here; I'm just curious in your opinion," Daphne persisted.

"I don't know, Daphne. Here's what I do know: Bottom line, no matter how she behaves around different people, she still has lymphoma; she will still continue to grow weaker, lose her appetite, sleep more, and eventually she'll be gone as a result of her lymphoma. How long that will take is not up to me."

"Yeah, but she acts so alive and normal." Daphne could not let it go; she needed reassurance.

"Daphne, give Kendera a break. She can't tell you what only God Himself knows. Besides, she's still here, so let's just enjoy her while we can, okay?" Kendra tried to wrap an arm around her sister, but it was shrugged off as Daphne reached for the nurse.

"You two, no wonder Kathleen wanted you here; you bring a smile to anyone's face, even under the worst of circumstances." Kendera gave them both hugs and reminded them to call if they had any other questions.

"Well, I'm off too unless you need me to stay, Kendra."

"No, we're fine. I know you have a lot to do today. I'll call if I need your help."

Having quiet time again, Kendra found she couldn't sit still. She needed to share her discoveries with someone who would care. She tried calling Blake and ended up only leaving a message. She didn't want to leave her thoughts on voice mail. Since Blake was not available, she called Sandy. After describing the previous day and the night to her friend, she expanded on the discovery that puzzled her the most.

"You know, Sandy, Mom has a personality style that fascinates me. While it's obvious I have a lot of her traits—okay, maybe that's putting it too strongly—while it's obvious I take after her in some respects, it is more blatant that she has a level of compassion I do not have. In fact, it would never occur to me to behave as she does. I know I've said this before; it's just weird to me that it is so strong in her. Make sense?"

"You have compassion, Kendra. Why do you always think you don't?" Sandy asked.

"Mom is very much concerned with dignity. When I think of dignity, I think I may be getting it confused with pride. Maybe they are a little too similar in my mind, maybe in hers as well; I just don't think so. Dignity is important to Mom, not just for herself, but for others as well. Dignity to her is making sure that nobody thinks ill of her. It is ensuring she is worthy of respect and treating others like they are worthy of respect. Because she often calls herself stupid or refers to her speech or actions as stupid, I have to wonder if she was either called stupid or made to feel stupid most of her life, and that may be the stem of this emphasis on dignity now."

"Gee, I don't hear anyone else saying they're stupid. No, that's unfair. You don't say you're stupid; you just say you don't have a lot of things that you really do. You say you're not compassionate, and yet you are. You say you're not a care-giver, and yet you are. Maybe it's just another way you're like your mother and won't admit?"

"It's not the same thing. Mom not only changes her story based on who is in the room, she changes her behavior. Did you realize that we do that too? Maybe we don't do it for dignity reasons, maybe we do." Kendra paused to find the right words. She was struggling to convey her discovery to Sandy. "It's weird, even sleeping most of the time she is still very much in tune with what others need to hear. Maybe she can see or sense the fear in those around her. Maybe she feels that everyone is stopping by to see how close to death she really is, and for that reason, feels she needs to either feed that curiosity or calm the fear in a dignified manner. Am I making sense?"

"Yeah, I get what you're saying. We all do that to some extent. We make a decision to either interact with someone or to just withdraw until they go away. Usually it depends on our mood I think."

"Maybe. I couldn't decide if this was a conscious decision by her or if it is just her personality. There is a personality type that is so concerned about others, you rarely see or hear them refer to themselves or do for themselves. I think I have always attributed that to a more introverted, feeling type person like you."

"Yeah, right, because I'm so shy."

"However, I would not say that Mom is introverted in the least. What I don't know is maybe she really was long ago. Maybe she's taught herself to be more outgoing and now appears to be an extraverted person."

"Well, that's not me, I've always been outgoing."

"You know, I've always attributed the word *caregiver* to her, just like I do to you. She had all these foster children and children of her own, and she cared for the elderly and pets; it's not a stretch to say she needs to take care of people. I never thought of it in terms of dignity, though, until today." Kendra was silent for a moment, remembering. "When I think back on how she cared for those elderly people, she treated them with dignity. She preserved their dignity in the process. I think most people in her life have missed this aspect or have chosen to just not look at it. Let's face it, to most, the dramatic, negative, who-did-what-to-whom is way more interesting than discussing how Mom was able to gently help someone to a sitting position while leading them to believe it was their efforts that got them there and not her. I know I wouldn't have thought about it before now. I know I'm rambling, and if you don't have time, that's okay."

"No, keep going. I have time."

"Okay, if you're sure," Kendra continued. "I got to thinking that these are the type of values that the world just doesn't dwell on anymore. How often do you hear someone refer to a friend, colleague, or family member as noble? I had to look it up; it means 'of an exalted moral or mental character or excellence.' Do you know someone who would fit this description?"

"Not off the top of my head, except maybe you, my husband, and if I really gave it thought, I'd probably say my mom as well."

"I don't think I'm one, but let's not stop on that note. I can think of several off the top of my head, you being one of them, of course, my sister being one, and most definitely my husband."

"I knew I shouldn't have answered; you just took my answer!"

"No, great minds think alike is all." Kendra chuckled, "Seriously, if we truly value characteristics such as loyalty, integrity, morality, and respectfulness, then why do we spend our time sharing stories about disloyalty, lying, immorality, and disrespect? Mary Kay Ash always taught, 'What you think about, you bring about.' Many other philosophers have preached the same concept, things like the power of positive thinking, and yet the news and gossip still stays on the things people don't want in their lives. If we're thinking about them enough to talk about them, aren't we bringing more of it into our lives?"

"Makes sense to me."

"I have no idea how much longer Mom has to be with us. It could be weeks; it could be months; it could be days. Only God knows for certain. I have no idea. I just know that should I die naturally, I doubt I could be as dignified as Mom. I don't know if I could maintain that sense of respect. I would probably be sarcastic, rude, and downright mean every time I heard someone say, 'I'm so sorry' or, 'My friend died from a similar disease.' Not Mom; she just takes it in and has a genuine conversation about it. Not in a demeaning tone, not in a disrespectful tone, just a discussion between friends. She's fascinating, Sandy."

"I hear you, Kendra. I agree. I pray we can all act a little more dignified and treat each other with dignity."

"You're awesome, Sandy." Laughing again, Kendra felt the need to let her friend continue with her daily chores. "Thanks for listening to me ramble."

"You don't ramble, and I'm here anytime. Take care, and I'll talk to you later."

As the day came to a close, Kendra sat on the porch swing once again looking into the dark Phoenix sky. "Lord, help my thoughts be on the things that are important to You. May my discussions be on the topics of things You would have come true in my life. And please give me the courage and compassion that You have instilled so deeply within my mom."

Rising with the sun, Kendra sat on the swing before the weather turned too muggy, enjoying a cup of herbal tea. Luckily she had remembered to bring the phone outside with her in case anyone called. She did not want her mom disturbed. Like most days, the phone rang as soon as the chime clock finished the stroke of eight.

"Hello, honey," Kendra answered, seeing it was her husband.

"Hey, gorgeous. How's my beautiful wife doing? Miss me yet?" Blake's husky voice came over the line. Kendra reveled in his voice, allowing it to wrap around her like a warm blanket.

"Yes, I miss you mucho lots!" She laughed.

"You've been gone a long time. How's it going?" he asked on a more serious note.

"Tomorrow will make two weeks. I think in that time I have seen Mom go downhill even more each day. Jenny says I've already lost my objectivity. I told her I have not, and no, I'm not over analytical, and I'm not a person to weave a good story around a few small facts, like some people I know. I just enjoy watching, observing, and taking mental notes that may make the facts a bit more interesting. Wait…is that me I'm talking about, or is that my mom?"

"Hmm, could be either if you ask me," Blake said, teasing.

"Oh, that reminds me. I called Mom a Mortholic the other day. You know, a cross between a Mormon and a Catholic."

"Okay, what brought that up?"

"Because I noticed she loves her Catholic rituals. I can't tell you how many rosaries she has around this place. I think if she had the energy, she'd still be crossing herself today! She did it all the time when we were growing up. She'd say, 'Hail Mary, Mother of Grace, give me the patience to not kill these kids of mine.'"

"Knowing your family, I'd say she needed all the blessings she could get."

"Daphne was asking me if we, as Mormons, believed in Jesus Christ."

"What did you tell her? No, we believe in the moon and the stars and the gypsy down the road?"

"No! I told her the truth, or as much as she was willing to hear. I explained we don't worship the cross; we believe in the atonement. Then she asked why we don't have crosses in our homes. So I said again because we don't worship the cross. These conversations are funny. She thought I was being condescending, but really I was trying not to laugh. I reaffirmed to her that I don't judge her for having the crucifix or rosaries. I see them as a visual reminder to folks that Christ died for us. Mom loves her crosses, rosaries, and her picture of the Last Supper. That is the faith that Mom has, that she has demonstrated to me her entire life."

"Did she believe you?"

"I don't know." Kendra continued on a more serious note. "You know I think it's important to believe. I think it is faith that makes this life a little easier to bear. I know that my purpose in life is to have joy. I watch Mom some days, and I know she is not having joy. And yet she doesn't give up. It hurts her to bend down and pet the cat, and yet she does. It hurts her to get out of bed some days, and yet she does. I know I may grumble about work, then I watch her and know in my heart that she would trade all of her tomorrows for just one of my todays." Kendra had to stop. Her voice was cracking, and her eyes were filling with tears.

"Well, you inspire me, dear. It's your faith that keeps me going sometimes. Do you need me to come out there? Are you sure you're okay?"

"I'm okay, really. Last night I read the first three chapters of the Book of Mormon to Mom. I love the way that book starts: "I, Nephi, having been born of goodly parents…" I have been born of goodly parents, regardless of whether I've ever realized that before or been willing to acknowledge them as goodly parents. I hope my kids feel the same someday. I hope they believe on some level that they have been born of goodly parents. I know we're not perfect; that is where Christ comes in. We try though. We try every day to be a good model."

"You are a good model, Kendra. Maybe too good," Blake reassured her.

Kendra sat with a smile on her face. Suddenly that song that Julie Andrews sings in *The Sound of Music* popped into her head, so she broke out in song to her husband, "Somewhere in my wicked, miserable youth, I must have done something good."

"Funny, you're funny, dear. I love you. You know that?"

"Yes, I know that. I hear her stirring in there, so I should go. Have a good day."

Feeling lighter in her step, Kendra went in to her mom with a smile on her face. It was going to be a good day.

CHAPTER 14

"Must you be on the phone now? You sound like a broker, always rattling off numbers and percentages. You're giving me a headache." Kathleen's voice was strained and tired.

"Funny, I never thought of it that way, Mom. I'll get off the phone; it can wait."

They sat in companionable silence watching *The Andy Griffith Show* when there was a light knock on the door.

"Hello? Is my grandma here?" a small voice said.

"Oh, hello, honey. I'm right here," Kathleen replied as she leaned forward, trying to intercept the rambunctious three-year-old who came running into her apartment.

Kendra came around the corner to see the bishop's wife there with her three children. They had brought a plant with tiny red roses on it, along with some special drawings. She watched her mom's demeanor change. She was in heaven. This is who she was. The little boy wanted to play catch and kept throwing his Nerf ball in Kathleen's face. His mom tried to stop him, but Kathleen kept encouraging him.

"I'm not a good catcher, am I?" She laughed.

Kendra left them to visit while she went back to work on the laptop in the kitchen. Shortly after the children arriving, the hospice social worker arrived. Kendra kept an eye on the room and its occupants while she continued to work. After all her meetings were over, the children had left, and it was just Elaine still there, she shut down her laptop and joined them in the living room. As they visited they uncovered the fact that Elaine had been the social worker for Kendra's dad in the years prior. Elaine checked the living will and DNR that was taped to the inside of the front door and then returned to the glider rocker.

"So you're Mormon?" she started.

"Uh-huh. Thanks to that daughter over there," Kathleen replied, pointing at Kendra.

"I had a friend who was Mormon. He used to preach to the convicts."

"I know some brothers in my ward that do that."

"He always told me the best way to help people feel worthy and feel loved is to point out to them that Christ loved them so much he died for them. He strongly believed if Christ felt they were worth loving, then they are."

"That's right; I try to tell my son Mathew the same thing all the time," Kathleen added.

"He would tell me that we are children of a heavenly Father, and we have a divine nature that often gets convoluted and squashed in the ways of the world. What I liked the most was that he would always look me in the eye and say, 'Remember your divinity each day and know that you *are* loved, and even with all your battle scars, you are worthy to be loved.' And you know what, I believed him."

Kendra smiled. Kathleen was nodding off again. Looking at Elaine as she watched Kathleen brought warmth to Kendra's heart. She truly cared.

"I know what he means, Elaine. Blake saved me when I felt as if no one would ever really see me for me. I hope everyone finds that special person. I believe that my mom found hers with Dad and Dad with Mom. I know they are looking forward to the day they can be together again in eternity, in a perfected state. It helps to have this faith, and because I do, I can look at her and say, 'Godspeed' because I love them both so much."

"You're a good daughter. There's no doubt you take after your mom." Elaine got up and gave Kendra a hug and Kathleen a pat on the shoulder as she departed.

Throughout that day and the next Kathleen was disoriented. At night, just after taking her medication, she gave Kendra a half hug and said, "Okay, baby girl, make a note that as of 7:05 p.m. on September 6, 1909, I turned everything over to you."

Kendra simply smiled and accepted what her mother had said, noting that she was off by a hundred years. She chose not to point it out though. As Kathleen made her way into bed, she looked at Kendra closely. "Did I say 1909? I'm so stupid; I meant 1919."

"Of course you did, mom, and please stop saying you're stupid. You're not stupid."

She was asleep. Kathleen slept the night through and most of the next day. Kendra noticed that she was beginning to see people that weren't there or at least that Kendra herself couldn't see. At one point, shortly after

Daphne had arrived to visit, Kathleen began talking with her sister Jo as if she were right in the room.

"You've finally come for me, Jo."

"What do you mean, Mom?" Daphne asked.

"Don't worry, Daphne; she's been calling me Jo since she woke up this morning," Kendra added. "Just go with it so she doesn't get upset."

"I thought your father would come for me; I didn't think it would be you," Kathleen continued. "Don't leave me!" she called. "What are you doing?"

As Daphne reached out to reassure her Mom, Kathleen fought back, pushing Daphne's arms away.

"I'm just putting you to bed, Momma. It's okay." Daphne tried to reassure her mother.

"Who are you?" Kathleen asked, looking into Kendra's face.

"I'm Kendra."

Kathleen looked confused.

"You don't look like Kendera."

Daphne and Kendra exchanged glances, and then dawning hit.

"She thinks you're Nurse Kendera."

Turning to her mom, Daphne said, "Kathleen? My name is Daphne. I'm here to help you get settled for the night. Is that okay?"

"Oh, okay." Immediate relief shone on Kathleen's face. "Wait, I need my medication, I didn't take my pills."

"I have them right here, Mom. I mean, Kathleen." Kendra offered her the pills with a glass of water on standby.

"No, no, no. Those aren't right. Are you trying to kill me? Daphne! Daphne! Help me. She's trying to kill me."

Kathleen struggled against the arms once again as she tried to run away.

"Kathleen, calm down. Let's look, okay? Here, it says here on your chart"—she picked up a piece of paper—"that you're supposed to have these pills right here at this time."

"What are you doing? You don't know what I need. Kendra knows. I showed her. Where is she? Kendra!"

"Mom, I'm right here. I followed your instructions; see, there're seven pills, just like you showed me. These are your night meds."

"Oh, thank you, honey. These nurses are so nice, but they don't always get it right, you know." She bent her head low and whispered to her youngest daughter.

Trying not to laugh, Kendra agreed.

Kathleen took her medication and finally laid back to sleep for the night.

Shutting the bedroom door, Daphne turned to Kendra and gave her a big, smothering hug. "Wow! How are you going to manage her by yourself?"

"She's never been like this before. I'll call you in the morning if she wakes up this way. Or I'll call hospice," Kendra responded, not really returning the hug but not fighting it either. "I think she's in what my friend calls the twilight right now. That's a nice name for it anyway. He says that most likely she's able to talk to people on both sides. Isn't that a fascinating thought? Could be why she's called me Jo all day. " Kendra said,.

"I don't know, but it would be cool if she could tell us and us believe her! You sure you're okay for the night?"

"I'll be okay. Is Ronnie coming out soon? Aunt Edna or Aunt Ruby? Anyone?"

"Ronnie's coming in a couple days. The aunts probably won't make it; Aunt Edna is sick and Aunt Ruby doesn't want to come alone. Jo's daughter Diane mentioned she might come out tomorrow, but I don't know how. I haven't heard from anyone else. Is Blake coming out?"

"Yes! He's coming out this weekend." Kendra's face actually lit up when she answered. "We may trade places with you for at least a day or so if you don't mind. Maybe you and Ronnie can stay with Mom while Blake and I get away?"

"Sure, whatever you need, little sis. I'll call you when I get home. Love ya." And she was out the door.

After bringing Blake up to date with the day's events and posting to the blog for the family, Kendra crawled onto the air mattress that was beside her mother's bed for a long needed sleep.

"Mom, Mom, are you up? It's time to go; c'mon, get ready."

Kendra rolled over in her sleep. "What?" She slowly managed to open her eyes and was immediately frozen in place. There, in the bedroom doorway stood her sister Jo. She looked radiant, healthy. *Impossible*, Kendra thought. *You're dead.*

Jo didn't seem to see Kendra. She just kept calling to her mom. Kendra looked over at her mom and saw her sleeping, and yet she was getting out of bed as if nothing were wrong. "Okay, honey, give me a minute." And then it all went away. The room was dark again, Jo was no longer there, and Kathleen was sound asleep in her bed.

Kendra looked over at the clock. It was 2:00 a.m. Kendra lay back on the air mattress and wondered, *Who's the one on morphine around here, her or me?* Gradually, she returned to sleep. The next day she could not have told anyone if she had actually experienced the visit from Jo or if she had dreamed it.

Kathleen woke up in a refreshed mood—not in too much pain, not disoriented for a change. She was tired but awake.

Much to Kendra's surprise, Diane knocked at the door shortly after Kathleen was settled in her chair.

"Diane! What are you doing here? I didn't know you were coming." Kendra grabbed her niece and gave her a tight squeeze.

"I told Daphne I was coming. We drove all day and night," Diane replied, turning to make room for her three children and husband.

"This is my husband, Lonnie. Lonnie, this is my aunt Kendra that I've told you about."

"Nice to meet you, Kendra; she's done nothing but talk about you the entire drive." Lonnie shook Kendra's outstretched hand.

"Wow, husband, huh? How long have you guys been married?" Kendra asked.

"Not long. Just a few months."

"Hey, Grandma Kathleen, how you doing?" Diane bent down to give Kathleen a big hug.

"Diane? Is that you? And who are these fully grown kids? They can't be those little babies I saw not too long ago." Kathleen was alert and cognizant, a state Kendra hadn't seen in a few days.

Diane and her family got comfortable in the tiny living room and settled in to catch everyone up on the family back in Michigan. They were having a surprisingly nice visit when Kathleen started to drift off again. After watching her sleep for a few minutes, Diane stood and said it was time to go.

"What do you mean it's time to go? You just got here," Kathleen, suddenly awake, asked reaching out to hold Diane's hand.

"It's a long drive, Grandma, and I have to work day after tomorrow," Diane answered raising her voice slightly as if to keep Kathleen from falling back to sleep.

"You mean you drove all the way down here from Michigan to spend a couple hours and now you're driving back? Daphne's not here yet; she'll want to see you." Kendra said.

"I'll catch Daphne another time. I really just wanted to see my grandma one more time. I wanted my kids to see her one more time, and I wanted my husband to meet her."

"Wow! Thank you, Diane." Giving her a big hug, Kendra walked out the door with them to see them off.

When she returned to the apartment, Kathleen wanted to go lie down. She was trying desperately to stand from the chair but had only managed to slide to the edge of it. Helping her stand, Kendra positioned herself behind Kathleen with her walker in front, moving slowly they managed to get to the bed. Before Kendra could walk out of the room Kathleen called her back to the bedside.

"Will you read to me, honey?" she asked her daughter.

"Of course I will, Mom, anything in particular?"

"Whatever you feel like reading. I just want to hear you read."

"I got it." Kendra went to the kitchen and quickly printed off pages from her blog to read. She only chose excerpts that shared her opinion of what a strong, wonderful woman Kathleen really was.

As Kathleen drifted off to sleep yet again, she smiled. "They don't think I'm the worst parent on earth and they understand I'm human, with human desires, wants, needs, and failings."

As Kendra watched her mom disappear again, she thought, *We may doubt that we are ready for the task that God has in store for us. It's easy to suddenly remember our human nature and frailties when we're asked to do uncomfortable things. I'm so thankful for all the many angels that continuously lift us up and encourage us to be the person that God intended us to be.*

While Kathleen slept, Kendra cleaned the apartment and managed to get some work done. Suddenly there came a crash from the bedroom. Kendra ran into the room to find her mother on the floor, up against the massive dresser.

"Mom! Are you okay? What happened?" Kendra asked as she reached down to help her mother get back up. Kathleen could not provide a coherent answer. She was weak and disoriented. *Ugh, this is harder than I thought.* Kendra was trying to be as gentle as possible as she assisted her mom back onto the bed; it was a task that took more effort than expected. Even though Kathleen was losing weight, there was still not much size difference between them.

Kendra managed to get her back in bed after what seemed to be a very long struggle. As she turned to go, her mother reached for her.

"I want my chair," Kathleen said. "I can't be in here."

"You sure?" Kendra asked, somewhat dreading helping her mother move again. "Yes, I'm sure. I need my chair!" Kathleen seemed to be almost in a panic. Kendra looked in her mother's face and saw fear reflected in her eyes. The urgency with which Kathleen was trying to throw her legs back over the edge of the bed confirmed her assessment. Kendra took a deep breath and whispered a hurried but heartfelt prayer. Reaching for her mom, she said in an upbeat tone. "Okay, well let's get you to your chair then." She physically maneuvered her mother to the walker and then stood behind her, helping her walk to the chair. Once settled in, Kathleen drifted back to sleep.

Kendra lay on the couch beside her mom's chair, keeping an eye on her. She put a hand on her mother's arm and watched her breathing.

"Are you all right, Kendra?"

Kendra jerked. That was a man's voice. It was her dad's voice. The television was off. Her mom was still asleep. She looked around. "Hmm, I must be as wacky as she is…I'm fine, Dad." And she lay back down, slowly closing her eyes.

When Kendra awoke, Daphne was coming in the door. Kathleen was still asleep in her chair.

The sisters sat and discussed the day's events; they shared family stories and even counted the grandchildren to see if there were more boys than girls. Daphne was upset she had missed Diane and couldn't believe she had only come for a couple hours. As Kendra was relaying the story of Kathleen turning everything over to her in 1909, Kathleen awoke.

"I need to pee," Kathleen said weakly.

"Okay, Mom, I'll help you." Daphne helped her up and much in the same manner as Kendra had done earlier positioned herself behind her mom with the walker in front, helping her walk, or shuffle, to the bathroom.

"I can do it myself!" her mother said just before Daphne emerged through the bedroom.

"She can do it herself," Daphne repeated to Kendra.

"She's nothing if not stubborn and determined, Daphne. Gee, do you think she passed that on to anyone?" Kendra said jokingly. "I'm going to go check the mail; I'll be right back."

Kendra was no sooner out the door when Kathleen fell for the second time. She scraped her shoulder, which was going to leave a pretty bruise.

"Kendra! Help!" Daphne yelled.

"What?" Kendra asked breathlessly, having run back into the apartment from only a few paces away. There was Kathleen, crying on the floor.

"Kathleen? It's okay. Let's get you up." Daphne was crooning in her mother's ear.

Together, they managed to get her settled with medication again.

"It's time to call hospice again." Daphne looked at Kendra, pleading with her eyes to tell her she was wrong.

"I'll call them." Kendra turned from the room.

"Who's out there? Where are you going?" Kathleen asked.

Kendra turned and looked at Daphne and then her mother. Trying not to laugh, she said, "No one is here, Kathleen."

"Tell them they can't drill holes in my floor. I'll have to pay for that. Make them stop!" Kathleen was getting more anxious.

In the most respectful manner, with no laughter, Daphne sat on the bed and began talking with her mom. Kendra stepped out and called hospice.

"Hospice is sending someone over," Kendra announced as she returned to the bedroom. "Kathleen, do you want some water?"

"Are you kidding me?" Kathleen replied.

Smiling, Kendra looked at Daphne. "I guess that's a no?"

"Don't you lie to me; you know I hate it when people lie to me." Kathleen was looking at the space between Daphne and Kendra with the stern motherly look they both knew so well. Not wanting to get her more agitated, they listened to Kathleen's conversation with the space until a male nurse arrived from hospice.

"Hello, Kathleen, how are you feeling?" he asked, walking into the bedroom.

"Who are you?" Kathleen asked.

"I'm Nurse Ken. I just came by to check on you. Your daughter said you fell a couple times today. Is that right?"

"You called a nurse?" Kathleen said, looking over at Kendra. "Why? I thought you were a nurse?"

"It's okay, Kathleen; he's here to help us out."

Looking him over from head to toe, assessing him in an obvious manner, Kathleen leaned over and whispered to Kendra, "He's kind of cute. I think that other nurse likes him; look at her practically throwing herself at him."

Kendra was laughing now; she couldn't help it. She said, "Do you want me to tell that Daphne nurse to stop flirting with that good-looking nurse?"

"Shh...they'll hear you," Kathleen whispered again, trying to slap Kendra's leg.

Daphne, Kendra, and the good-looking nurse Ken from hospice proceeded to review the events. Ken suggested they order a bed alarm so they could be alerted if Kathleen tried to get up again on her own. He also asked if they would like a hospital bed brought in.

"You're not putting me in a hospital!" Kathleen yelled from the bedroom.

"She refuses to stay down!" Kendra said, laughing. "And her hearing is the best it's been in years!" Turning toward her mom, Kendra answered, "Don't worry; we're not going to put you in a hospital. We're going to get you a new bed though, one that people use with special back problems to help them get in and out of bed." Kendra winked at Daphne and the nurse.

"Well, why didn't you say so? Don't you put me in a hospital. You promised you wouldn't put me in a hospital." And she was asleep again.

"You know, Daphne, that's one thing Mom gave us that we can't deny," Kendra said. "She gave us the gift of laughter. She used to tell me jokes when I was injured, make me laugh when I was in the emergency room. I could be pouring out blood, and Mom would find humor in it. Now, I'm so grateful that she gave me that gift."

"That's going to really help you through this," Nurse Ken said.

"Exactly! Like she knew we would need this someday," Daphne added.

"I know we shouldn't laugh so much, but for me, life is about having joy and even though death is sad and depressing and empty and lonely, we know they go on. They go on different than we do, but they live."

Daphne and Kendra were walking Nurse Ken toward the door. Looking over her shoulder at Kathleen, Kendra continued, "They live in our hearts, in our memories, and in some spiritual sphere. So it's okay to find humor. Mom has nothing to worry about. "

"She's so lucky to have the two of you here," Ken said as he walked out of the apartment.

"Yeah, remind me of that when it's my turn and my kids are laughing at me," Kendra replied, closing the door.

CHAPTER 15

Kathleen's time was getting shorter, and Kendra knew it. Despite numerous conversations regarding her condition, the answers were always the same. Nobody knew how much longer. Everyone just knew that eventually the cancer would win, and she would be gone.

The confusion continued, and the attempts at humor grew. Daphne and Kendra attempted to care for their ailing mother—neither being educated nor trained in the fine art of medical care. They would accidentally spill water on Kathleen, force feed her, have engaging conversations regarding the ingredients of Tapioca, attempt to convince her she was improving while the entire time she drifted further and further from their reach.

Both sisters were amazed at the spirit that lived on within their mother. Each day she would still insist on getting out of bed in the morning. She would still insist on making her own way to the bathroom and caring for her own personal hygiene. On occasion, they would watch her just collect things to hang on to while she napped in her chair. She would collect the television remote, a box of tissues, pens, newspaper—anything that was within reach.

Kendera continued to assure them that the behavior they witnessed was normal. The patient was losing the battle, and she would subconsciously attempt to hang on to anything. "They want to be in control like anyone else," Kendera had said during one of her visits, personal hygiene is the last thing they relinquish.

Late in the evening, long after Daphne had gone home. Jerry showed up to visit his grandmother.

"Hey, I didn't know you were coming. You could have called me."

"I know. There wasn't time really. It was a last-minute decision."

"Did you have a good trip? How long are you staying?" Kendra asked as she hugged her baby boy.

"I'm only here for the night." Setting down his overnight bag, he sat on the edge of the sofa. "Grandpa died yesterday, so I want to be back for the funeral. Grandma's not having a service, right?"

"I'm sorry to hear your dad is going through this as well, and I'm sorry to hear about your grandpa. It must be hard losing your last two grandparents so close together."

"Jenny's there, not Janie. Is she awake? Can I go in?"

"She went to bed about an hour ago. Go on in."

Jerry made his way quietly into the bedroom. He was hesitant at first, allowing his eyes to adjust to the darkness. As he started to walk in, he heard his grandma call his name.

"Hey, Jerry. What are you doing here? Is your wife here? How's the pregnancy going?" Kathleen was alert and immediately engaged with her grandson. Kendra softly closed the door and allowed them their privacy.

When he came out over an hour later, he looked exhausted.

"You okay?" Kendra asked.

"Yeah. I gave her a blessing. I gave her Jenny's love too. Did Jenny tell you that she was holding Grandpa's hand when he passed yesterday?" Jerry looked wearily at his mother.

"Yeah, she told me she literally squeezed the last breath out of him hugging him after he had gone." A small attempt at a smile formed on Kendra's lips. Her son was worn down and in pain. She wanted desperately to ease that pain and yet understood she could not. It was the pain of loss. She knew his faith was strong and would see him through this tough time.

"Watching all this is like watching a small piece of what Jesus suffered at Gethsemane," Jerry stated. "He suffered through all the cancer victims, the diabetes victims—not just one type, all types! I hate watching her go through this. Can you imagine having to watch Him go through it, knowing he was doing it for you?" Jerry searched his mother's eyes.

"Jerry, I'm thankful to be here now in her final days. I know she is not living each day in fear of dying; she has accepted it. I am touched, impressed, awed, surprised, enthralled, and truly fascinated to watch Mom each day as she refuses to give in. I only pray that I am as strong as her and that you never have to watch me go through anything like this." Kendra hugged her son, and together they shared the tears of sorrow that would live in their world for a short time.

The next morning, Jerry left at dawn to return for his grandfather's funeral. Daphne arrived shortly after with Ronnie. They caught up as sisters and brother while their mother slept.

"It's been what, a year and a half since Daphne first called with the diagnosis? I looked it up, read about it, but never, ever imagined what I see today. How about you, Daphne?" Kendra inquired.

"You know me; I studied it and studied it. I still don't think she's at the end. She's got months left. Kendra keeps trying to end it early for her," Daphne replied, holding her brother's hand.

"Is that right?" Ronnie asked. He was a big man, well over six feet tall. He was quiet, with soft brown eyes and thick rich dark hair. His baritone voice resonated in the air even though he spoke softly. .

"You know, in all the preparation Mom did for her own death, she made sure that none of us kids held her medical power of attorney," Kendra added.

"Why's that?" Ronnie asked.

"Because she didn't want us to have to make the call to take her off life support and end her life. Can you imagine thinking in that detail when you're faced with your own end?"

"No, but then I never really think about it as being an end," Ronnie replied.

"I can tell you I underestimated what I was walking into this time. Not that I would trade this experience for any other in the world. This time is so very precious to me. I get to see a side of Mom I wouldn't have seen otherwise. I cannot believe her strength, will, and determination."

"What's this?" Ronnie asked as he grabbed a box with his name on it.

"That's your stuff. Everything Mom set aside for you." Daphne volunteered.

Together, they sorted through papers, cards, letters, and memories.

"Wow, I can't believe she saved all this." Ronnie was choked up, clinging to a letter he had written to his mom years and years before. "I guess some folks might think I'm being silly."

"No, Ronnie, they wouldn't," Daphne said, comforting him.

Kendra sat in the glider-rocker studying her brother and sister as they sat beside each other on the sofa. At one time, she and Ronnie had been in the same algebra class. He had received straight As while she had struggled to understand the concept. Not once had he offered to help. *And I never asked*, she thought. *After all these years, I still remember that? Why can't I remember the happy times?* Returning to the moment, Kendra interrupted them from their reminiscing.

"For me, it was a heart opener." Kendra said. "I was cleaning out a drawer and found countless clippings of advertising for Daphne's store and Keith's garage." Keith was the oldest brother that never left the small town they had grown up in. He was also quiet and withdrawn from the family. It was a trait the brothers seemed to share.

"You did?" Daphne asked.

"Yes. I also found old letters, cards, newspaper articles, and pictures from people I had no idea she stayed in touch with."

"Did you read them?" Ronnie asked.

"No, I haven't read them yet. I don't have to read them to know what is in them." Reflecting on the experience, Kendra added, "Each letter must have been written in response to one they received from her, one that was written by hand, not typed. Each letter was written with love, concern, and curiosity to know the other person. Each letter had her time invested in it—time to write one, time to read theirs—caring to save it, and love to keep it."

"I never thought of it like that," Ronnie said. "Personally, I don't write."

"Yeah, we kind of gathered that, bro," Daphne said, giving him a small push with her shoulder.

"Watching Daphne take care of Mom, Ronnie, is so touching. She has so much patience. She asks a thousand questions, which is funny. But then she always asks a thousand questions."

Chuckling, Ronnie agreed.

"Seriously though, the love and fear in her eyes, in her voice, and in her touch is prominent. Maybe that extra bite of pudding will cure Mom and she'll be her normal, funny, strong, confused self by tomorrow."

"You force-feeding her, Daph?" Ronnie asked.

"No! She's hungry. Kendra's starving her."

Looking over at Kendra for the expected playful response, they saw the acceptance instead. Kendra's voice was soft and low as she continued, obviously not having heard their interjection. "And then I realized we won't see that woman anymore. She's been unable to speak properly for days now, and yet I can hear her clear voice in my head saying my name, calling me honey, asking if I'm okay, if I'm hungry, if I need anything, a blanket, a drink, a hug, a kiss, anything. And now she can't even form the words." Kendra had to stop. Once again, the reality of losing her mother soon was tearing her apart. She was no longer able to hide it.

"Kendra, when your heart is heavy with the sorrow and the loss that will soon be experienced, it becomes difficult to find the joys. Right now she sleeps. She sleeps in peace. The Lord is with her acting as her blanket and her shield. He can do more than we ever can." Ronnie reached out to hold her hand, he couldn't stay strong. His tears were flowing as freely as both Daphne's and Kendra's.

"She doesn't want her blanket pulled up past her knees, nothing on her face, nothing weighing her down. She frequently stops breathing, for a beat or two. Her breathing is very rhythmic, so it's obvious when it stops."

Daphne was shaking her head no to Kendra's words. "She's just tired; she gets like this."

"Today may be the last day that I can hold her. It may be the last day I can hold her water for her and encourage her to drink from a straw. Today may have been the last time I could hold her hand." Kendra focused on her siblings for support. "I held her hand today, but she didn't hold mine. She only held mine if I used both hands to hold hers, using my hand to close her fingers around my other hand. She did slap at me though." The memory brought a small smile to Kendra's lips. "And she reached for me. She reached for me to help her. I was her support. Our two bodies were one as we walked from her chair to the bathroom to the bed."

Taking a deep breath, Kendra decided to stop being so solemn and get back to business. "I spoke to her bishop today, so I would know what to expect and how to plan closure for her friends."

"Bishop?" Daphne asked. "You didn't call a priest? I can call one."

"Why a priest or a bishop? I'm here," Ronnie interjected.

Kendra laughed. "And here we are. I called her bishop because she's Mormon. If you need a priest here, Daphne, then call one. Ronnie, if you need privacy, then by all means, take it. Let's not fight, though, when we all believe the same basic principle—that Christ died for us. Okay?"

"You're right, Kendra. A friend of ours told me that even though we know we're supposed to rejoice and be happy for them, sometimes we just can't. It's the selfishness in us that gets in the way. I'm feeling selfish right now. I want my mom healthy and happy and out here saying silly things to us. But it's not our decision. It's His," Daphne said.

"I'm sorry. I don't mean to demean anything from your beliefs, either one of you. It hurts me to see this outer shell of who she is, and I'm sure it hurts you too. Why don't you go in and see her, Ronnie? I'm going for a walk." Kendra dried her eyes and grabbed her cell phone as she walked out the door. Once she had found refuge near the fountain at the pool of the complex, she sat down and dialed her husband.

"Hey. Whatcha doin'?" she asked in a tearful voice.

"What's wrong?"

"I'm okay. Ronnie is here, and we were just all talking, remembering. I can't wait to see you. You'll be here tomorrow?"

"Yep. Don't tell your mom though; she might leave before I get there." He chuckled.

"You know, for the first time in all of this, I think I see all too clearly—clearer than I want to see." She sat silently for a moment, watching the water fall from the fountain. "Even though I've been able to state facts and do research, I guess I've been in my own form of denial. The day the disease would win would just never get here. Or somehow it would get here, and I'd be okay."

Kendra sniffled. Collecting herself, she tried again. "I'm not okay. I don't want to lose her like this. Even though I know that I'll see her again. Even though I know that there is an eternal life and that she will no longer be in pain. Even though I know that she'll be with my dad and sister, I don't want her to go. Not now. And yet I don't want her like this. This is not her. She's trapped inside this dying body, unable to speak clearly, unable to express her thoughts, her desires, her questions; unable to convince that body to stay in routine and do what it needs to do each day. Her soul is frustrated and is seeking a way out. It is unable to live until this body dies."

"I'm sorry you're going through this alone and I'm not there yet."

Not really hearing his response, only his voice, Kendra continued to think aloud.

"I thought I understood how her days must have been taking care of Dad. I wasn't even close. The fear of waking up to see if they're still breathing. The fear of leaving the room in case they need you. The fear of being unable to ease their pain or inadvertently making their pain worse. The loneliness she must have felt. Unable to take a shower because he might need her. Unable to walk to the mailbox in case he cried out. And considering the demands a loved one can make when they're healthy I'm sure are only intensified when they are frustrated and trapped." *I ignored her.* Kendra didn't want to say that out loud. The pain she was feeling because of her guilt was eating at her. She needed to get this said, and she knew Blake would understand.

"I feel remorse for not being there more frequently when my dad was dying. For not offering to relieve her for thirty minutes to take a shower and do her hair. For being so caught up in my own life that I never gave a second thought to how hers must be going each day. For over eight months she cared for him while he died a little each day. I've been here almost three weeks, and it's breaking my heart. The pain that must be associated in watching your husband go through this. You know, it doesn't matter how many people are around, when you die, you die alone. She is the only one experiencing this awful disease. I'm only watching the effects."

"I know," Blake said softly.

"The love she felt for Dad is so evident now. I know she loved him. I've always known she loved him. I'm so blessed to understand the depth of that love at this time. As it breaks my heart, it opens my heart. Like when you work out. In order to get bigger muscles, you need to work them, which actually tears them so they can grow. My heart is tearing so it can grow right now." Kendra broke out in uncontrollable sobs.

"I'll be there tomorrow. Hang on. Okay?"

"I'm okay. Really. I'm sorry to do this to you. Just the sound of your voice calms me. I can't wait to see you." Kendra took a few deep breaths and concentrated on the breeze, the birds, and the water flowing in front of her. "I'm better now. Thank you for letting me get those thoughts out. I'm sure I can sleep now. I love you."

"I love you too. See you soon."

The next day brought a new level to the downward spiral. Kathleen was no longer able to stand on her own. When she opened her eyes, they had that vacant quality Kendra had seen in her dad. Then it was as if she would return after blinking several times. Even then Kendra couldn't be certain until she saw Kathleen reaching for her baby boy.

Watching her reach for Ronnie, Kendra could see the frustration in her eyes; she could see the pain in Ronnie's as he watched her watch him. Kendra watched his eyes fill with water and remembered hearing her mom call them her baby boy's big beautiful brown eyes.

Kathleen turned her gaze to Kendra. It was as if her mom was pleading with her. *Is she in pain again? When was the last time she had her meds?* Kendra checked the paper they had been using to keep track of her medication. It was time for more. Kendra interrupted the interlude between Ronnie and their Mom to administer the medication and then left them to their privacy.

Shortly after she had walked out of the bedroom, the people appeared with the hospital bed. Daphne, Ronnie, and Kendra arranged the furniture so that Kathleen's bed was beside the mechanical bed. They couldn't openly call it a hospital bed because it would upset Kathleen; instead they referred to it as the bed used for special back pain patients. Kendera stopped by and visited for a while trying to convey her sympathy. She increased the medications for Kathleen, per the doctor's order, to keep her comfortable.

Daphne sat with Kathleen and held her, kissed her, and kept saying, "I love you, Mom." No one wanted to leave her side. It was obvious to all that it was the last moments. Whether they be hours or days, Kathleen was nearing her end, nearing her peace.

Kendra watched her sister and brother. For the first time she saw how different they were from what she remembered. All those years of thinking they were in competition, only to discover that they were so similar. They shared the same fears, the same passions, and the same intensity in all they did. More importantly, they shared the strength in Christ. Not only was she getting the benefit of learning who her mom was and seeing her courage and tenacity, she was also getting to see her sister. She could watch Daphne's kindness, her gentle touch, and her eagerness to please. She saw who inherited that from their mom. She smiled.

Now, after spending weeks with her sister, she was getting to see her brother, not as the older brother that either ignored her or teased her but the man—a man that was about to lose his mom, a man with love in his heart and tenderness in his touch.

I wonder, in watching all of this, if this was me instead of Mom, how would my children be behaving? Would they be too busy fighting over their own values and paradigms rather than trying to see my life from my eyes? Would they be caught up in passing judgment on family members rather than enjoying the decision they had made? Would they be respectful of the relationships I had formed?

Looking at the clock, Kendra saw it was time to pick up her husband. She had anxiously been awaiting his arrival. Excusing herself she headed off.

When their eyes met across the aisle, her breath caught. As if in a dream, Kendra walked straight to Blake and enveloped him in her arms. He tightly wrapped his around her and held her close. *Too bad we can't stay this way forever*, Kendra thought as they made their way to baggage claim.

Kendra was snuggled up to her husband as they drove back to the apartment from the airport. "The logical side of me is fascinated even while my heart breaks. Most times I'm able to focus only on the logic, the reason, the analysis. Occasionally though, that heart side of me just gets too full and takes control. I guess we all have that desire to be understood at our deepest places. To be justified in our feelings. I hope and pray that I'm close to Mom's." Looking over at Blake, she noticed the straight-faced expression he bore. "I'm sorry. I'm rambling. I haven't seen you in almost a month, and now I can't stop talking about sad things."

"You're allowed," Blake responded.

"I'm just thankful that I can still get up on my own. That I can walk myself to the bathroom, pick up a cup of water, swallow the drink of my choice. These are such small simple pleasures we have in life. Our independence. Not all forms of independence take a war to win. Sometimes, it's won through humility and the grace of God."

Blake rested his hand upon her thigh and kept his eyes on the road. Kendra closed her eyes and breathed in the comfort he exuded.

Shortly after reaching the apartment, Ronnie and Daphne left promising to return the next day. Blake and Kendra were able to relax for a short time before the nightly routine of medications and soothing began.

The next morning Kathleen awoke just before Daphne and Ronnie appeared. She was back and she was energized. She pushed herself to the edge of the bed, sitting up on her own. That was as far as she could go. While she rested there, Ronnie entered the room.

"Where are you going, Mother?" He smiled while leaning over her to give her a hug and kiss.

"I'm hungry."

"Okay, we'll get you something to eat. Want to go sit in your chair?"

"Oh, yes, please. That would be wonderful!"

Ronnie swooped her up in his arms and just carried her to the chair.

"Oh, don't hurt yourself; I must weigh a ton!" Kathleen squealed.

Daphne came out of the kitchen with some applesauce. "Here you go, Momma, food. Here's applesauce; just open up and let it slide down." Daphne was quick on the spoon. She was so happy to see her mother acting normal again.

Kendra stood back watching, taking in the scene and monitoring her mom's reactions. After about thirty minutes Kathleen started getting agitated and confused. Feeling it to be her role to be the bad guy, Kendra stepped in.

"I think we need to back off and let her breathe."

"Wait, just one more bite!" Daphne exclaimed, pushing a Popsicle in her mother's face.

"Why don't we go to Starbucks or something, dear?" Blake asked as he intercepted his wife from the crowd.

Glaring at him and then looking at the hope her sister's eyes and a look she perceived as agreement in her brother's, Kendra replied, "Fine. I get the hint," She didn't really want to leave, but she didn't want to stay either, so she allowed her husband to escort her out. Once they were in the car, she continued her internal chastise.

"Did you see her? Did you see the look on Daphne's face? Do you think they don't recognize this for what it is?"

"And what is it?"

"It's probably her surge like the book says. Just yesterday she was talking to the two boys and the cute little girl who left their toys everywhere; other than that I guess she's perfectly normal."

"Yes, I saw her."

"She woke up late last night calling for Jo."

"And?"

"You know what conclusions I've come to?"

"Several, I imagine."

Ignoring his attempt to lighten her mood, Kendra responded. "First, repetition breeds complacency. I say this because initial reactions are always so dramatic. We pay so much attention to detail; we jump at everything. Then after days and days of the same thing, we become complacent. We think, 'Oh, just that again.' We take our time; we don't jump as frequently. I mean, think of your first day on the job and then after several weeks or months?"

"And second?"

"Second, guilt should not be dished out based on location alone: I've listened to most people call my sister and ask her, 'What do you think?' or, 'How bad is she?' Okay, folks, it's called *terminal cancer* for a reason! Daphne is not a doctor, and she does not make your decisions. How dare they call and put that burden on her! She called last year; she called earlier this year; she called again when Mom was put on hospice; how much more is her responsibility? Why can't anyone be sensitive to her feelings and not put the burden of their decision on her? If they waited too late, that is on them, not her. Right?"

"Agreed."

"Third, does your identity really need to be known to enjoy being sweet? Mom was so sweet the other night! All night! I don't believe I've ever known Mom to be so sweet for so long. Maybe it's because she doesn't know who we are; maybe it doesn't matter who she thinks we are. She made the sweetest comments. We'd ask if she wanted some water, and her response was, 'Oh, that would be wonderful!' Or when we asked if she needed her medication, 'Please, oh, please, may I?' Her voice, her tone, everything about her was so sweet. Should it really matter that she had no idea who we were? I don't think so. She just pulled Daph down and gave her a big kiss and said, 'Oh, you treat me so much better than my daughters.'"

Blake didn't respond; he didn't even look at her. Feeling the need to get it all out of her system, Kendra couldn't stop herself.

"And fourth, the roller coaster has just begun, me thinks…oh, I pray it's about over. Then I feel guilty for wishing it over. We are officially in the stage of 'I don't know.' Each time she awakes, it's a different person. It may be the mom that is independent and demands to sit up." Kendra changed her voice to imitate her mother. "'Get these blankets off; I want to be in my chair!' Or it may be the mom who cannot sit up, can hardly speak, and is just in a lot of pain. Today it was the mom who was hungry and talkative. We just never know who is going to wake up each time. I can honestly say, though, each one of them requires a lot of attention, patience, love, understanding, calmness, touching, soothing, *argh*!

You know me; you know what all of this takes and how hard it is for me. I'm not saying I can't do it; I'm simply saying I have to apply thought and energy. It is not something that just comes naturally, routinely, or without thought." Kendra paused, her balloon truly deflated.

Blake was silent as he drove. Kendra knew he was driving nowhere in particular, just as long as they were out of the apartment. Obviously, this is what she needed.

"See how much I'm growing, dear!" Kendra exclaimed.

He laughed at her. She laughed at herself.

"I can tell you that it's getting more difficult to concentrate on anything. That could be a combination of lack of sleep and too many people demanding consolation. Like I said last night: you ask, I answer, and sometimes I do not have the energy to think before talking. I do that about every three to four hours when Mom wakes up. Then, listening to Daphne—my goodness, she can talk! I don't know how she does it. How does she come up with so many details to talk about? It must be a woman thing!"

"Yes, dear," Blake answered in his purely supporting tone.

"Where are you taking me anyway?" Kendra asked, just realizing that they were leaving the city.

"We're going to the mountains, to Daphne's house. You can rest a little, get a couple hours sleep, and just relax with your hubby. That okay with you?" Blake smiled lifting his eyebrows at her in that familiar Groucho Marx fashion.

"Absolutely, dear." Kendra relaxed and laid her head on his shoulder to enjoy the remainder of the drive.

CHAPTER 16

Kathleen was acting more and more restless. She was never really able to differentiate who was in the room and who wasn't, which seemed to add to her frustration and confusion. She looked exhausted, as if she were physically battling some unknown enemy. Only the enemy was known, and it had a name.

Nothing Kendra did seemed to help. Kathleen was in the twilight, telling her dad that she would feed the baby and sounding frustrated because someone wouldn't give her the baby. She kept asking where people were, people Kendra had never heard of before. Kendra watched her siblings try to comfort their mom. To her it felt as if death were taunting, teasing, flirting even. *It's not enough for her to want it, she has to need it. She has to desire it so strongly she's willing to reach for it, giving up control of her last instinct. It's as if death were floating in and out, stealing her breath and then returning it one more time, staying just out of reach yet calling to her. It's playing hard to get to increase her desire, increase her need, and decrease her control.* Perhaps it was a living thing, and yet it promised to take her, on its own schedule, after her will was gone.

Kendra and Blake were at wit's end; all night they had wrestled with Kathleen. Even though they had taken turns, neither one had managed much sleep. Daphne and Ronnie had arrived early while Kathleen slept. Kendra explained to them that Kathleen had been upset the entire night. Finally, after family deliberation, Kendra broke down and called hospice again.

After talking with them and explaining the events of the night, the doctor took her off one medication, leaving her on just two. The nurse came by the house shortly after the phone call to check on the patient and the family. Nurse Kendera was unavailable, so another nurse attended.

"She has nothing coming from her right lung—no sounds, no breath, nothing. Her left lung has fluid in it, which is creating difficulty swallowing. You can use these swabs to rinse her mouth, and it's probably best to give her the morphine right in the pocket of her cheek."

"How much longer are we looking at?" Daphne asked. "She still has a while, doesn't she?"

"According to the book," Kendra said, trying to rescue the nurse, "this indicates maybe days or hours."

"Well, nobody knows for sure, but it's probably safe to say that we're looking at the end soon. How long soon is, we have no idea."

After the nurse left, Ronnie and Daphne were in the living room watching television or reading. Kendra and Blake sat outside near the pool just enjoying the misty spray from the fountain nearby.

"As weird as it sounds, I wouldn't trade this time for anything," Kendra revealed to her husband. "People have been e-mailing me and calling me, thanking me for doing this. Wow, the thought of being thanked for this never occurred to me. Mom asked; I accepted. I felt it was something I could give her, something more than a card or a trinket, something real and heartfelt. It was never about anyone else, just Mom. I truly feel I'm blessed to be here. Did you hear me start singing to her last night?"

"And I always thought you loved your mom!" Blake teased.

"Ha, ha. I know I can't sing, but I'm sure she didn't mind. The words from 'How Great Thou Art' were just in my head, so I started singing. I sang parts of songs I could think of, any song. It brought a smile to her face. Who cares if I can't carry a tune? I can bring a smile to Mom's face, and that's enough."

Blake squeezed his wife.

Silently they sat and watched the other tenants move about the complex.

Breaking the silence, Kendra continued with her thoughts. "While watching her struggle, I wondered, Is this our hell? Is this the time we spend working through the wrongs in life? The wrongs we may have committed and never reconciled?"

"Could be."

"If so, I'm a little scared of it. I can imagine that it could be a pretty awful place. Or maybe it's the place we go to fix things we didn't have or didn't have the way we thought we should have had them. Either way, I think it's a place of longing, longing to correct things or make amends. Maybe it's a place where we long for death. That death requires us to give in and give up. Something we are taught to never, ever do. We are taught to fight, to survive. Maybe that's why Mom can't let go yet even though she's ready. What do you think?"

"Maybe." Blake was noncommittal. Kendra knew Blake was just letting her talk out loud. He did that often, as if he knew it was the only way she had of working things out in her head.

"Let's head back. As nice as this is, I don't like being away long."

Holding hands, they walked back to the apartment. As they walked in, Ronnie was joining Daphne in the bedroom. Blake and Kendra followed him.

"I need to go feed my animals," Daphne said, watching her mom sleep. She was peaceful. "I don't know if I should leave though. What do you think?" She turned to Kendra for an answer.

"Go. I'll call you if anything changes."

"You sure?"

"Go!"

Ronnie collected their things and agreed with Kendra. Everyone needed a break, and this could go on for days. He had extended his trip home by two days already and had to leave in the morning. Kendra knew he wished he didn't have to, but there was just no telling, and his wife and daughter needed him back home.

He hugged and kissed his little sister good-bye, he told his mother good-bye, and he shook Blake's hand as he walked out the door.

"You sleep tonight. I'll give your mom her medication. You're up every two hours; you need your sleep," Blake told his wife as he tucked her into the bed beside her mom's.

"I'll probably wake up anyway, but okay. Have I told you how much I love you lately?" she asked as she squeezed his hand.

"No, but you can later." He winked at her, planting a light kiss on her forehead.

"You know, with death so close, it becomes easy to begin thinking about tomorrow. Death is close enough, and until it beats her, until it breaks her will and ends this mortal existence, she is alive and with us. Thanks to the atonement; it can only win this physical body and not over our spirits. Not where it really counts, not who we are."

"She's not really with us anymore, you know that?" Blake asked tenderly. "She's gone more than she's here. You're doing everything you can, so don't you feel guilty about anything. You hear me?"

"I know, I know. Death prolongs one more day for now. Until it wins, I'm just going to lie here and hold her hand, talk to her, sing to her, whisper to her, rub lotion on her, change her, clean her, whatever it takes to make her comfortable and make her feel the love that is in her home. "

"And I'm here to help you; now go to sleep!"

Kendra slept most of the night. Blake administered the medications as needed throughout the night. Waking up in the early morning, she watched her mom sleep and listened to her breathing. It was shallow, slow, and very unsteady. She reached over and placed her hand in her mother's hand.

Kathleen awoke and started making awful moaning sounds. It was a heart-wrenching moan. Since she was unable to verbally communicate, Kendra couldn't determine if it was pain or just not being able to speak or if she was somewhere in another dimension. It sounded horrid. As Kendra sat beside her to administer medication, Kathleen opened her eyes. Her jaw was moving; she was trying desperately to speak. Her eyes pleaded for something. Kendra felt so inadequate and so wrong. She felt that anything she did was only causing her more pain and misery. She felt like she had let her mother down. Her mom's biggest fear in all of this was the pain, and now Kendra felt like she had failed her.

Kendra reached for a cool cloth and washed Kathleen's face and neck. She washed her hands and gently rubbed lotion on her arms, constantly wiping away both hers and her mother's tears. Blake entered the room and asked her if she was in pain; to their surprise, Kathleen moaned, and it sounded as if she answered, "Uh-huh." They gave her more medication since the prescription was as needed, an instruction that had Kendra feeling more inadequate. Kendra asked her if she wanted her gospel music, and again she moaned, "Uh-huh."

Kendra put in a DVD just outside her bedroom doorway that was interviews and singing of her favorite artist, Vestal Goodman.

Blake was with her on the bed and saw her tilt her head, trying to see the television. He came and pulled the television out a little for her to watch. She seemed happy.

Throughout the day, Kendra would go in and wash Kathleen's face, wiping gunk from her eyes, cooling her skin, arms, legs, and chest. Her eyes always bore into her daughter with a silent plea, a plea that Kendra could not comprehend.

Kendra wasn't sure if her mom really saw her; it felt like she could. In desperation, she called Daphne and explained everything that was going on. Daphne reassured her sister.

Unable to tear herself away, she cleaned and filed her mom's nails; she held her hand, washed her face some more, put face cream on her, and talked to her the entire time. Kathleen would stop breathing for thirty-five to forty seconds out of every minute. Blake sat with Kendra, monitoring the breathing, watching his wife. Together they watched Kathleen struggling for each breath. Only she looked so peaceful.

After what seemed like hours, Kendra's cell phone rang in the other room. She hesitated to leave but finally relented. It was work and nothing terribly important. Now that she had left the bedroom, though, she felt a need to work for a while. Do something other than watch and worry. Blake sat in the living room, and the DVD played over and over.

Blake's cell phone rang, and he stepped outside to take the call, trying to keep it quiet in the house and not interfere with the music. Kendra walked in to check on her mom on her own way to the bathroom. Kathleen's breathing was shallow, rapid, and not quite as raspy as it had been earlier.

As Kendra came out of the bathroom, she immediately saw that her mom was no longer breathing, and she knew. As she approached the bedside, Blake came around the corner.

"She just stopped," he said.

"She's gone. The nerve of her, waiting until I was in the bathroom! That's exactly what my dad did to her! How dare she!" And while she tried to joke, she started to tremble. Blake held her. After several moments, her logic kicked in, and she pushed Blake away.

"We need to clean her up and call everyone."

Kendra could sense his hesitation to let her go, but it was what she needed to do. She would hang on to this efficiency until it was all over and then she would cry.

Kendra called Daphne first since she knew it would take her almost an hour to drive down. Daphne said she would call the family if Kendra could call hospice and their older brother Keith. Kendra assured her she could, asked her to drive careful, and hung up. When she spoke to hospice, she asked that they delay in picking her mother up explaining that her sister needed time to get there and say good-bye first.

While they waited, Blake and Kendra cleaned Kathleen, changed her clothes, closed her eyes, and got her presentable. And then Kendra just sat beside her.

"I'm so sad to see her leave and yet so relieved she's gone. Does that make me a bad person?" she said to no one in particular. Blake did not answer; he simply put his hand on her shoulder and squeezed her gently.

"At least she won't be struggling for air or moaning from pain or unable to maintain her dignity because her body just won't support her anymore. She had such a hard life; she deserves some peace and rest."

I need to call Keith, Kendra thought. Reaching for her cell phone, she looked at Blake for strength. "I need to call Keith while I can still talk calmly."

"I know."

"Hello, Keith?"

"Yeah, who's this?"

"It's Kendra; you busy?"

"Well, if you're calling, then I guess she finally kicked the bucket, huh?"

"Yeah, Keith, she's gone."

"Figures; it's my anniversary today."

"Well, consider this your anniversary present then." If Kendra could have slammed down the cell phone, she would have; instead she simply hung up.

Daphne arrived shortly before the mortuary employees. Kendra was in shock. No tears, no emotion at all. She watched as the people from the mortuary covered Kathleen's face with a sheet. She hated seeing them lift her mom from the bed and put her on the gurney. Before she could comment that her mom didn't want her face covered, they uncovered her face. They were very professional. Keeping her dignity, not exposing her in any other way.

Kendra stood and watched while Daphne cried. Over and over in her head she repeated, *You're free now, Mom. No more pain. You're free. I miss you so much. I wouldn't trade these past weeks with you for nothing. I'm so very thankful I got to hold your hand, wash your face. I'm grateful I got to sleep beside you and give you comfort. I am even more thankful that I got to say good-bye. To touch you, fix your hair, give you one last kiss before they take your mortal body away. Lord, keep her safe.*

Kendra looked around the apartment, knowing that soon it would no longer be hers. Everything would be gone. All the material things will be dispersed, and only her memory would remain for those who stayed behind.

Kendra reached over the dresser and removed a locket that Kathleen had given her and told her not to wear until she was gone. The locket contained a picture of Glenn and Kathleen on their wedding day.

With one last kiss good-bye, Kathleen was rolled from the apartment. She was gone.

CHAPTER 17

The next days were a flurry of activity—phone calls to agencies, visits to the mortuary, closing for her friends, and emptying the apartment.

While Kathleen had not wanted a service, Kendra remembered the funeral she had attended the previous year and the importance of getting closure for those left behind. So she arranged for a very small celebration of life at the local ward that her mother attended. It was only her close friends, Daphne with a few of her closest friends, and of course the bishop and his family.

Kendra made all the appropriate calls, closed accounts, and made all the necessary arrangements. Blake and Daphne helped her as much as possible while trying to stay out of her way. Jerry and Melissa drove out with a trailer and took most of the furniture, even the curio cabinet for his sister Janie. Kendra made no comment regarding the curio cabinet or the fact they were taking most of the furniture. She just kept moving, organizing, and planning the next steps to closure.

She felt rushed. She felt as if the vultures were swooping in to partake of their prey, and yet she knew they weren't. They were all going out of their way to give her room to do what she needed to do. Blake had to fly home soon, and Kendra was looking forward to the nineteen-hour drive alone. What didn't fit in her car, they stored in Daphne's garage or attic until another time.

When it was all said and done, Kendra and Blake sat at Daphne's kitchen table the eve before their departure.

"I can't believe it. I've gone through everything—bank accounts, safety deposit boxes—and she barely had anything to her name. It's sad to think after seventy-six years of working so hard, there was nothing left."

"Whatever you found you should donate to the animal shelter in her name," Daphne volunteered.

"I can't. That's for each person to decide. I'll send out everyone their portion, and they can decide what to do with it or how to spend it. Thank you for taking Missy, by the way. I don't think she would have gone to anyone else."

"Yeah, well, we were real lucky to have found that lady who wanted Callie. I know Mom would rather have seen her cats put down than go to a bad home. I don't think I could have done it. Could you?"

"Yeah, easy for you to say; you don't have the scratches from that stupid cat!" Blake almost whined as he displayed the said scratches up and down his arms from catching Callie. It had not been a fun event. They had to corner that poor cat in the bathtub and wrap her in a towel in order to get her in the carrier. If she didn't stay with the lady who wanted her, then she was on her own. Fortunately, both the elderly woman and Callie found what they needed in each other.

"It's not over, you know. The storm has come and passed. All day I've heard the words to that Reba song in my head. "Clock's still ticking, life goes on…I guess the world didn't stop...for my broken heart," Kendra said. Quoting movies or songs made it easier for her to express how she felt.

"No, the world didn't stop. The chores still need to be done; cats still need to be fed; laundry needs to be washed. Speaking of which, I need to go out and feed my critters before they whither away." Daphne smiled as she headed for her barn shoes.

The next morning, after dropping Blake off at the airport, Kendra drove away. She recalled leaving her mother's apartment the day before. *This is the end of my adventure in Phoenix and the beginning of a new adventure somewhere else.* She remembered walking into the bedroom and still feeling her mother there. It was still her room even though the only items in there were the curtains and her empty dresser. *Is it because it's where she breathed her last breath? Is it because it's where she spent her last days? Or is it because it was the room most hers? The bedroom, the room where we really relax and be ourselves. It's the most personal space we have. Is that why I still felt her there even though all her clothes were gone, her wall hangings, knickknacks, books, bed, everything, gone. How did I still feel her there?*

Leaving was harder than she had anticipated. With each passing mile, the stress shifted from being an executor of a will back to being an employee and having her own work to catch up on. For once she had felt like an equal, like an adult, not like the baby. Now she was leaving it all behind. *Is this a moment in a time,* she wondered.

Or did it change the relationships with my brother and sister forever? Only time would tell. She felt drained. She wondered how she would find the strength to give of herself to the people who needed her when she didn't want to be around anyone. She just wanted to be left alone, given the bereavement she was entitled to. And yet she was afraid to grieve, afraid she would give up and get lost in the sorrow.

The drive was wonderful. It was quiet, and it provided plenty of time for Kendra to focus on her feelings of introspect, wondering how her mom's departure would affect lives going forward. *What will change*, she wondered. *Something will.* Something always changed, but not her faith. She could be sad and rely on her faith as usual. She knew that her faith would get her through this and anything that life threw her way.

Kendra realized that life doesn't stop for grief; it continues in full force, demanding attention and contribution. After catching up at work, she had a friend's wedding to help prepare, followed by the birth of a new grandson. Then came the sad goodbyes as a loved one went off to war in Afghanistan, followed by a new granddaughter. Then, Jenny was in a car accident. While she suffered from whiplash, it was not as bad as it could have been for which Kendra was grateful.

There were knee surgeries and broken bones; and life continued to happen.

Occasionally, Kendra would find herself lost in sadness. She would watch movies and cry silently—something she had never done in the past. She was involved in her cosmetic business again and tried to focus her energy on her customers' needs. She felt numb, though, lost in the emotion of loss and trying desperately to let go and let God.

Blake walked in the house one afternoon and heard his wife crying. Following the sounds, he found her sitting in the middle of the all the pictures she had carried home from her mom's apartment. He walked in and sat down beside her and put his arm around her. She just turned and leaned into him, sobbing. She was feeling broken, and all he could do was hold her.

It had been over eight months since her mom had passed away, and still she mourned. She had been slowly withdrawing and shutting down; now she was letting it out. She cried for several minutes before attempting to excuse herself from her husband.

"It occurred to me when a parent dies, the circle moves forward, and the next generation moves up to become the parent. The next generation becomes the grandparents or whatever role is there to fill. With Mom gone, my generation is now the parent, the very parent I used to go visit, and when I would visit, I would go through the family picture albums. I now have those albums, and my children and grandchildren will go through those albums and new ones. Before long, I'll be gone, and my children will be the parent kids come to visit and so on and so on." Kendra cried into Blake's shirt, using it as a tissue in the process. He held her and kissed her temple.

"I miss Mom. I look at her pictures now and weave a wonderful story around them, a story that emphasizes the qualities she instilled in me, a story that will go on for generations. No, she is not gone. Only her physical body is gone. But I still miss her."

Blake held his wife and whispered a small prayer for God to help her heal, that He would walk with her in Texas as He walked with her Phoenix, that he would uplift her and send the angels her way to bring out the woman everyone saw but her.

Sitting outside between the trees as the sun slowly rose over the barn, Kendra held her cup of herbal tea in both hands and allowed her head to sink over the back of the chair. There was a slight breeze and a chill that would warm throughout the day. She didn't feel the chill, just the breeze. She breathed the fresh air deep into her lungs and slowly released it.

"Whatcha doin' up so early, beautiful?" Blake's deep voice startled her.

"Just enjoying the sunrise. What about you?"

"I missed my wife."

They sat in silence for a short time before Kendra had to share her excitement. With a smile on her face, she started the details. "I realized last night that I need to call Keith. I owe him an apology."

"You were hurting and his comments were callous; why should you apologize? Shouldn't he apologize to you?"

"Maybe, but regardless of what he needs, I know I need to apologize. I also know that eventually I'm going to have to face this estrangement with Janie."

"Why's that?"

"Last night I had the most wonderful dream. Once I woke up, I immediately wished I could return. Never can I recall awaking so alert, so refreshed, and so knowing that even if I tried for another hour, I would not return to sleep or to that dream. It was the most wonderful feeling, a feeling I know I'll never have again if I don't make things right."

She looked to Blake to see if she could read his mood. He was sitting there with so much love in his eyes Kendra couldn't help but smile bigger.

"In my dream I went to visit my parents at their home in south Phoenix. This was the home Mom sold around 2001, shortly after Dad died. In the home were both my parents, my sister Jo, a baby, a dear friend of my parents, a priest by the name of Father Paul, my parents' dog, and their two cats. We were all in the living room. We were laughing and carrying on. Dad and Father Paul were playing practical jokes on Mom. Jo was laughing her familiar cackle while patting the back of a baby, which was lying beside her on the couch. The house was bright, cheerful, warm, sunny—a place that we see in advertisements but never get to really experience.

"It took some time for me to notice that they were all very young, vibrant, energetic, glowing, and just amazing looking. When I finally commented on it, my mom laughed and said, 'Oh, honey, we're so glad you came to visit. I'm sorry you can't stay, but we'll see you soon enough, I guess.' I began to protest because not only was I feeling better than I could ever imagine, but I loved being with them. And I didn't just want to be with them because they were my parents but because of the atmosphere, the love, the warmth, and the laughter. The second time Mom said I had to go, I awoke, which was immediately followed by my thought, *No! I want to go back!*

"Every being in that dream, with the exception of me, has died. The baby took me some time to figure out. Then I recalled that Jo had a baby who was born with a hole in his heart and lived only seven days. I know that was the baby Jo was patting in my dream.

"Isn't it a wonderful thought? Wouldn't that be so cool if that was my little peek into heaven? To know that we will be restored to a beautiful, healthy body; that we will have light spirits and so much love. And to know that we can be together for eternity, as a family, and know that we are bound in that love.

"That dream has brought me such comfort, Blake. Daphne mentioned the other day that even she had a dream of Mom. All she really remembers is Mom was very youthful and healthy looking. Don't the Scriptures promise that we will be given a perfect body? That is how I saw everyone. They were perfect."

Blake smiled at his wife and relaxed with his own cup of tea. He reached over and set his hand on her thigh, giving it a light squeeze. He joined her in looking off into the sunrise. "Yes, dear, that would be wonderful."

listen|imagine|view|experience

AUDIO BOOK DOWNLOAD INCLUDED WITH THIS BOOK!

In your hands you hold a complete digital entertainment package. In addition to the paper version, you receive a free download of the audio version of this book. Simply use the code listed below when visiting our website. Once downloaded to your computer, you can listen to the book through your computer's speakers, burn it to an audio CD or save the file to your portable music device (such as Apple's popular iPod) and listen on the go!

How to get your free audio book digital download:

1. Visit www.tatepublishing.com and click on the e|LIVE logo on the home page.
2. Enter the following coupon code:
   1bbb-3e2c-f989-94a3-a434-f488-ae4d-9950
3. Download the audio book from your e|LIVE digital locker and begin enjoying your new digital entertainment package today!